ONE SMALL ST
ONE QUA
FOR M

Theorizing that a man could time travel within his own
lifetime, Dr. Sam Beckett stepped into the Quantum
Leap Accelerator—and vanished.
Somehow he was transported not only in time, but
into *someone else's* life. . . .
And the Quantum Leap Project took on a whole new
dimension.

QUANTUM LEAP

Now all the excitement and originality of the
acclaimed television show are captured in these independent novels . . . all-new adventures, all-new leaps!

OUT OF TIME. OUT OF BODY.
OUT OF CONTROL.

QUANTUM LEAP

LEAP

THE WALL

A NOVEL BY
ASHLEY McCONNELL
**BASED ON THE UNIVERSAL TELEVISION
SERIES "QUANTUM LEAP"
CREATED BY DONALD P. BELLISARIO**

ACE BOOKS, NEW YORK

Quantum Leap: The Wall, a novel by Ashley McConnell, based on the Universal television series QUANTUM LEAP, created by Donald P. Bellisario.

This book is an Ace original edition, and has never been previously published.

QUANTUM LEAP: THE WALL

An Ace Book / published by arrangement with MCA Publishing Rights, a Division of MCA, Inc.

PRINTING HISTORY
Ace edition / January 1994

ISBN: 0-441-00015-0

ACE®
Ace Books are published by The Berkley Publishing Group,
200 Madison Avenue, New York, NY 10016.
ACE and the "A" design are trademarks
belonging to Charter Communications, Inc.

PRINTED IN THE UNITED STATES OF AMERICA

10 9 8 7 6 5 4 3 2 1

ACKNOWLEDGMENTS

The author gratefully acknowledges the support and assistance of Kathryn Ptacek and suggestions and support from Anna Nusbaum, Phyllis Linam, Bill Davis and other habitués of GEnie, and Lynn from Northgate Technical Support. In addition, she would like to express a debt of gratitude to her mother, who never, ever threw anything away, and to her sister, who held the memory that started it all. This one is yours, Mom, and yours, Mary Pat.

QUANTUM LEAP

THE WALL

HEADQUARTERS
7100TH SUPPORT WING
WIESBADEN AREA COMMAND
INFORMATION AND INSTRUCTIONS FOR
NONCOMBATANTS IN THE EVENT
OF AN EMERGENCY

3. **ALERT SIGNALS:** The signal for an alert will be a five (5)-minute rising and falling blast of the sirens in the Wiesbaden Area (not to be confused with the one (1)-minute rising and falling blast sounded Monday noon for test purposes or the less-than-one (1)-minute steady blast of district sirens for calling police and fire officers to routine duties). In addition, an airplane will fly low over the Wiesbaden Area firing double red flares.

4. **ACTION UPON ALERT:**

a. In the event of an alert all noncombatants will:

(1) Return immediately to their quarters.

(2) Assemble the items listed in paragraph 5 below. . . .

(3) Await further instructions . . .

(4) If not contacted . . . within two (2) hours of the Alert Signal, proceed to the Eagle Club.

(*cont'd.*)

CHAPTER

ONE

"Children should quickly learn the fact that their misbehavior can cause their fathers to suffer official humiliation."
—Innumerable guides to military life

By now he knew what it felt like to Leap out of someone's life, had learned to recognize the moment of completeness, of rightness that precipitated the lunge Out.

But he would never, never learn how to prepare for the Leap in. He never knew if he would end up in the body of a pregnant woman, a retarded teenager, a college professor, or his own best friend. Or even himself. He never knew if he would find himself in the middle of giving a college lecture or in the aftermath of making love, of catching a pop fly or flying a fighter jet.

Or, as now, absorbing a blow that sent him reeling back against a wall. He was aware of the impact of flesh against flesh and flesh against wall, of a deafening shriek, and the smell of juniper berries.

Bar fight? he wondered, holding a hand to a lip, feeling blood, bunching his muscles to uncoil in self-defense.

Another blow, and he found himself sprawling. *Must be one hell of a big guy*, he thought muzzily, staggering up again.

The shrieking was resolving itself into words. The dark blur in front of him was becoming a figure, an impossibly tall backlit shadow with a lifted hand. Despite himself he ducked back, fell again.

"Don't you talk back to me!" the shriek was saying. "Damn you, don't you talk back to me!"

He opened his mouth to say, "But I'm not," then thought better of it. It wasn't in his best interest to argue with a giant.

The hand before him dropped suddenly, and the shriek was replaced by a sob. The giant fell down before him on her knees, and when the hand was lifted again it was to brush clumsily at his brow. "Missy, Missy honey, I'm sorry, Mommy's sorry, don't cry honey, Mommy didn't mean it. Don't cry."

Mommy? Missy? He glanced down at himself, as much to get away from the alcoholic fumes as to check and see who he was this time.

"Oh, nuts," he whispered. He was wearing a dress again.

The stroking hand paused. " 'Nuts'? *'Nuts'?*" The hand pulled back and descended again in a lightning-quick slap, at too short a range to have much power behind it, but strong enough to rock him back again. "You get to your room!" The woman heaved herself to her feet, staggering, and extended one unsteady hand to point the way. "You get in there right now, you hear me, and you don't come out again until I tell you!"

He was tempted to crawl, to stay beneath and out of range of that threatening hand, but something wouldn't let him, and besides, he could move faster when he was on his feet and knew what to expect. He scurried down the hall and ducked behind the indicated door, closing it behind himself with a sigh of relief.

4

His face was beginning to hurt, and he was certain that he had a bruise on the back of his head where he'd hit the wall. He couldn't feel any other injuries.

From the other side of the door he could hear weeping.

He wondered if he should be crying, too, instead of feeling—what *did* he feel, anyway? Bewildered, certainly. Shocked. A sick feeling that there must have been a reason, that he—no, not him, it couldn't have been him, he wasn't even there—that someone must have done something to cause that sobbing, those words, those blows. There had to have been a reason.

But reason or not, there was no possible excuse. And the emotional reaction there was easy to identify. Taking a deep breath and letting it out again, he decided it was anger.

Never, in the opinion of a good-natured quantum physicist, a very constructive emotion; one he had always felt faintly ashamed of. But this was one of those rare occasions when even Sam Beckett felt anger was fully justified. With a muttered curse, he let fly with a spinning kick at thin air.

And landed on his rump, tangled in a rag rug.

He'd been right the first time. Anger was not a constructive emotion.

Struggling to his feet again, rubbing the tender place on his posterior, he finally took a good look around the room.

A twin bed, with a pink bedspread.

A picture of a Disney Alice, having tea with the Mad Hatter and the March Hare, hung on the wall over the bed. He snorted in sympathy at the confused look on the cartoon character's face. Alice didn't know the half of it. The headboard was white, with imitation gilt paint in imitation plasterwork. A chain of plastic daisies hung from one of the bedposts.

A pink plush stuffed doll, with a plastic face and threadbare patches, was propped carefully against a lace-edged pillow.

He turned slowly.

There was a window, with tiny plastic horses perched on the windowsill. A small bookcase, stuffed to the gills with very thin books. A miniature dresser next to a full-size one.

The miniature dresser came complete with miniature mirror. Taking a deep breath, he steeled himself and stepped into square with it and looked at the person reflected in the frame.

She was a very pretty little girl. About six, he judged. She had long brown hair, neatly parted and braided, with bangs cut severely across her forehead, and she had lovely violet eyes. He blinked, fascinated to watch the long lashes moving, and blinked again. It took him a moment to realize that he couldn't see her blinking.

He couldn't watch himself blinking, because his eyes were closing too. His eyes, which were her eyes, which were almost the color of the bruise rising on the side of her face. He raised a hand to touch, carefully, and the little girl in the mirror winced.

So did he, and not just at the stab of pain from the cheekbone. Sam Beckett had always considered himself the flexible sort. Adaptable. Versatile.

But he'd never been a six-year-old girl before.

"Oh, boy," he said.

Verbeena Beeks straightened up and folded her stethoscope neatly into the pocket of her lab coat. The man in the bed stared at her, wide-eyed and silent, and Verbeena shut her eyes briefly and sighed. A whimper of apprehension came from the bed, and the doctor opened them again and smiled brightly.

"Hello there! My name is Dr. Beeks. What's yours?"

His hands clutched at the sheet covering him, and he sneaked a look past her at the white walls, the eerie blue light. "Is this a hospital?" he whispered. His voice was oddly high pitched to the doctor's ears.

"It's a kind of hospital," she agreed, making careful note of the pitch. Sometimes it was difficult to identify the Visitor, and every clue helped. "What's your name? You didn't tell me."

"Is my mommy here?" He looked around again, clear apprehension in his eyes.

No mirrors for this one, Verbeena decided. *No reflective surfaces, even. This is a really young one.* "You didn't tell me your name, honey."

"Missy. My name is Missy. M'lissa Renee Robicheaux," he said, pronouncing the words carefully. "Where's my mommy?"

"Melissa?" Verbeena choked. Not only a child, but a girl child? It took her a deep breath to recover enough to say, "That's a very nice name. How old are you, Melissa?"

"Missy," he corrected instantly, and then flinched, his gaze darting around the white room as if looking for someone. "I'm six." It was a whisper.

"Well, you're a very big girl for six years old," the doctor said. *Oh, Lord. Sam, where are you now? What have you gotten into this time?* "This is . . . this is like a hospital, Missy. You need to stay here for a little while."

"Do I have to get a shot?" His hands—long, elegant musician's hands—twisted around each other.

"No, honey. No shots here." She smiled and patted the sheet.

The wary gaze snapped back to her, as if assessing, and then he asked cautiously, "Can I have my Susie?"

Verbeena dredged her memories of her childhood. "Is Susie your dolly?"

A flash of fine indignation: "Susie's my *friend*. I'm too big to have a dolly."

"You certainly are, dear." Verbeena sighed again. This one was going to be very, very complicated. "I'm afraid Susie isn't here right now, and we weren't, um, expecting you. Do you—" *how to put this*—"do you know where you live?"

"Einundswanzig Texasstrasse, apartment five. Major Robicheaux's quarters."

The recitation was flat, without that quality of "affect" that the doctor was used to in her involuntary patients. It took her by surprise. "I beg your pardon?"

"Einund—"

"No, no, that's all right. I heard you the first time." Missy cringed, and Verbeena changed the subject hastily. This one was afraid of anything that looked like criticism. "Do you know what town you're in, honey?"

"Hainerberg." Once again, there was no emotion. The words had no meaning for the little girl. "Is my mommy coming soon?"

Hainerberg? Where the hell is Hainerberg? Verbeena wondered. She shrugged; she could always come back to it. Meanwhile, let Ziggy, silently monitoring, take the data and run with it. "And when is your birthday, Missy?"

"This month!" He smiled, a smile to break her heart. "I'm going to be six whole years old this month!"

"You mean, you aren't six *yet*?" *This is even worse than I thought.*

"Almost! I almost am!" He cringed, pressed himself back into the bed, away from her. "I didn't lie!"

"No, no," she soothed, a terrible suspicion beginning to dawn in her. She paused, mentally adding up the flickering gaze, the twisting hands, the shrinking away from her shadow, even the repeated requests for her mother, the response to perceived corrections.

8

At six, surely she should be more independent? "No, you didn't lie. I'm not mad at you, honey." She reached out, carefully, and took one of his hands in hers, patting it gently. "Nobody's mad at you here, I promise."

He relaxed minutely, and the doctor reached out to brush the lock of white hair out of his eyes. His gaze never left her hand, as if he expected her to lash out without warning.

"Tell me about yourself, Missy," she said. "Tell me about your family. Tell me about Hainerberg."

"Al, I'm really worried about this one," she said two hours later in the main conference room. "This could be very, very bad."

The small dapper man across the table from her rolled an unlit cigar back and forth in his mouth. "Bad? How bad can this be? He's Leaped into a serial killer, for God's sake. He's been pregnant! How much worse can you get than pregnant?"

"I'm sure he found it a very soul-enriching experience, Admiral," Verbeena said, glaring. "Pregnancy is a wonderful thing. Having a child you've wanted and loved and planned for . . ." She paused. Sam Beckett had certainly never planned to be pregnant. Shifting gears, she went on, "That isn't the point I'm trying to make here. Dr. Beckett has had quite a lot of experience by now with Leaping. I'm more worried about our guest."

"Why? She won't remember anything. They never do. It's that swiss-cheese effect. Plays hell with Sam, but I always figured it worked in our favor with the guys he traded places with." Despite the title, he was not in uniform; he was wearing civilian clothing. Defiantly, vividly civilian clothing.

"This is not a guy, Admiral."

Her repeated use of his title instead of his name finally penetrated, and he realized she was really annoyed. He took out the cigar and leaned forward.

9

"He's been a woman before."

"This is not a woman, Admiral. This is a *little girl*. A *very* little girl. And any minute now she's going to realize that she's in the body of an adult male. Al, this is . . . this is a kind of child abuse." She chewed her lower lip. "And the worst thing . . ."

"Child abuse? *Sam*? Are you nuts?" Al was on his feet and pacing, his arms flailing like windmills. "Sam Beckett would no more—"

"I realize it isn't his choice, Al, but what's going to happen to that little girl? If she remembers *anything* about this, it will scar her for the rest of her life." She took a deep breath and let it go. "And the thing is, I'm afraid she may already be carrying some scars. I think Missy Robicheaux may already be an abused child."

CHAPTER
TWO

"Though there is no apparent rank among wives,
tradition and courtesy expect proper recognition
and respect to be accorded those whose husbands
occupy positions of high responsibility."
—*Protocol, Officers' Wives Club*

Sam could well imagine that it was taking Al and
Ziggy a while to figure out where and when he'd
landed this time. He still wasn't sure himself. The
hours shut up in the bedroom stretched on. Looking
out the window, he could see two rows of identical brown buildings, rectangular, three stories tall,
facing each other across a narrow street. A scattering of saplings in full leaf dotted the lawn between
them. It looked like a young, grim housing project.
The street was almost completely free of traffic. He
spotted a handful of cars in diagonal slots in front of
the buildings; they were massive and blunt, station
wagons mostly, dating from the mid- to late Fifties.
Well, that gave him some idea when he was, even
if he didn't know for sure *where* he was yet.

The angle of the sun felt wrong for the season the
trees showed. All that told him, really, was that he
wasn't in the same latitude he grew up in; you could

take the physicist out of Indiana, but you couldn't take the farm boy out of the physicist. He watched the shadows stretch out and listened to the sounds on the other side of the door and wondered what on earth he was supposed to do this time. Report being slapped? To whom, and how?

A man with a leashed German shepherd came around the corner from the next building over. Sam leaned forward, straining to see; the dog wore a heavy muzzle, and resisted the lead. The man yanked him along impatiently, clearly wanting to get this "walk" business over with.

Finally, the dog began sniffing at a convenient bush, and the man stood still, checking his watch impatiently. Sam could sympathize with the dog; he was beginning to feel a reminder of liquids past himself. The dog had just lifted his leg when, from a loudspeaker some distance away, came the sound of a trumpet.

Sam watched with amazement as the man stiffened in place, yanking the dog away from the bush, and remained at strict attention as the trumpet—a scratchy recording—played "Retreat," and then the National Anthem. The man did not relax, nor allow the dog to finish, until the trumpet was silent.

The man and dog circled the building and disappeared. Sam sighed, put his elbows up on the windowsill, and rested his chin on his doubled fists. After a while a pair of children crossed his field of view, heading toward the end of the building, followed a few minutes later by three more. He could hear the faint sounds of children shouting, and wondered idly what games they were playing.

His train of thought was interrupted by a brisk pounding at the bedroom door. "Missy! You get out here and wash your hands and set the table!"

With relief, Sam headed for the door, pausing only long enough to let Mrs. Robicheaux disappear down the hall. The location of the bathroom was a wild guess that proved to be a lucky one; he closed the door behind himself and faced the same problem he seemed to face every time he Leaped to the opposite sex: a mind wired for one set of reflexes in a body configured for another. Fortunately, by this time, he had learned to compensate and adapt to the physical requirements of the body he occupied, whatever they might be. Though fastening a bra behind his back was still something of a challenge, as he recalled. Fortunately or otherwise, Missy was too young to worry about *that*.

A brown wooden step, obviously handmade, was next to the sink, ready for a child to stand upon. Washing his hands afterward, he studied the bruise reflected in the mirror. It was darker now, and ominous looking. Sam shook his head, carefully—sudden motion made his head ache—and checked the rest of the child's body with clinical thoroughness, looking for other signs of abuse.

There were a couple of faded yellow marks along her ribs, and a more recent, greenish one on her leg. There were beatings, then, but not every day. Sam suspected that they might be a result of the mother's drinking, and the paucity of old bruises and scars might mean that she had only just progressed to attacking her daughter. That might mean that he had Leaped to somehow short-circuit the cycle of child abuse. He hoped so. He found himself liking the little girl whose body he occupied, even though he had never—would never?—have the opportunity to meet her in person.

Well, he might, someday. Sam had given up predicting the future about the time that the past had gone berserk. It didn't matter, anyway. He would do what he was supposed to do, Leap, and . . . do what he was supposed to do.

"Story of my life," he murmured to the child in the mirror.

"Missy? Did you fall asleep in there?"

13

"No . . . Mom," he answered, scrambling to respond.

At the other end of the hallway from the bedrooms was the living room, dining room, and kitchen. Two doors at the far end of the living room led to a closet and, presumably, an exit.

His pell-mell rush came to a screeching halt as he registered what rested next to the door. He looked over uncertainly to find the woman—now that he knew he had Leaped into a child, he realized that she wasn't really a giant—reaching into a china cabinet, getting out a set of cut-crystal glasses.

He looked again, gave the living room a quick scan. Yes, that was a tired-looking overstuffed green couch against the far wall, and a massive leather club chair, battered from years of use. He couldn't see a television set anywhere, but a cherrywood cabinet in the corner had four large doors and stirred a faint memory, as if the Beckett family might have had a similar cabinet, back in Indiana. He wasn't sure, but the sight of it gave him a pang of homesickness.

Over the couch, a mountain landscape in an ornate frame held pride of place. On the floor, a loose carpet that had once been red covered the floor. An elaborately carved, dark coffee table held an empty crystal candy dish and a squared-off stack of magazines and newspapers. He made a mental note to take a look at them as soon as he had a chance. They'd give him details about where and when he was.

And lined up next to the door, waiting, were three large suitcases, and three quart bottles of water.

Nothing in the scene went with cut-crystal glassware.

"Are you going to stand there all day?" the woman said sharply. "Snap to!"

"Yes, Ma'am!" he responded, startled.

From a corner of the kitchen, a boy of perhaps ten sneered at him.

Uh-oh, he thought. *I'll bet a girl's big brother isn't any better than a boy's big brother*. And then he recalled, with a start of guilt, that he had been a girl's big brother once upon a time, as well as a boy's younger sibling, and wondered if this Leap wasn't Someone's way of paying him back for some of the tricks he'd played on his little sister Katie.

"Dammit, Missy! How many times do I have to tell you to move! Are you deaf?"

She was a woman of forty years and average height, not slender and not stocky, her blonde hair short and badly permed, her hands red about the knuckles, her dark blue eyes lined, her face ill and tired. Just now she was clutching the top of a dining room chair as if it could keep her from falling somehow, pressing it back against the flowered shirtdress.

He cleared his throat. "Mom, are we . . . are we going away somewhere?"

Missy's mother closed her eyes. "No. Not unless they call the alert. I explained all that to you. Now set the table, unless you want a spanking."

Sam moved around her warily—nearly tripping over a voltage transformer in the process—keeping out of striking range just in case, and noticed gratefully that Missy's putative brother was taking knives, forks, and spoons out of a drawer and putting them on a countertop. He dived for the silverware, and began to move around the table, putting it in place in front of the chairs. There was one more chair that needed a place setting. Missy's mother left the kitchen and walked slowly down the hall, her hands at her temples.

"You're gonna get in trouble, you're gonna get in trouble," the boy sang off-key. The kid had the same brown hair Missy did, the same violet eyes. He was thin and wiry, dressed in a long-sleeved shirt and

15

gray slacks. He got up on a step stool and opened a cupboard, getting out three plates. Sam wondered if those long sleeves covered the boy's share of bruises, too.

Three? Only three? Sam wondered. He was beginning to wish Al would show up. There were a lot of questions he'd like the answer to, questions he couldn't ask. Like, for instance, Where's Daddy?

"She's gonna tell Daddy on you, and you're gonna get it when he gets back," the boy said, as if answering him.

Sam made another trip out to the dining room, carrying plates, and back again. "When's he coming back?" he asked, as casually as possible. *How does a six-year-old girl sound*? he wondered desperately, suddenly realizing another pitfall of this particular Leap. He couldn't for the life of him remember what his little sister Katie sounded like when she was six.

The boy started to answer, then stopped. "That's a secret," he said, stirring something in a pot on the stove. He moved around the kitchen as if he were well used to putting a meal on the table without the assistance of an adult. Sam wondered just how often Missy's mother hit the bottle, and how hard. He was still wondering when the telephone in the living room rang, a shrill double note.

The boy raced out to answer it.

"Major Robicheaux's quarters, Tom speaking, may I help you?" he recited breathlessly. Sam blinked. So Missy's brother was named Tom. Sam's own older brother was named Tom, too. Interesting coincidence. And this was Major Robicheaux's quarters. And a ten-year-old answered the telephone in a way that would put many a professional secretary to shame.

Tom laid the handset down carefully and yelled, "Mom! It's Colonel Baker's wife!"

Mrs. Robicheaux came back, still pale. She picked up the phone, paused to take a deep breath, and

16

said cheerily, "Doris? How nice of you to call."

Sam thought she didn't look very pleased, though. The circles under her eyes were more pronounced, and she kept rubbing her temples.

Tom had paused in carrying a platter of pot roast to the table, and was openly watching his mother. Mrs. Robicheaux, catching sight of him, turned away. After a short conversation she hung up the phone.

"Is it the Russians, Mom?" Tom said, his voice tense and oddly adult.

"Don't be silly, Tom. It's just the Officers' Wives Club meeting."

She said nothing more, even when Sam, reaching for the pepper and misjudging the length of his arm, knocked over his glass of milk during dinner. Tom flinched, but Mrs. Robicheaux only sighed, squeezing her eyes shut as if to deny the entire scene. Sam hopped out of his chair and ran for a dishcloth to clean up the mess, and the meal continued in silence.

Afterward, he got up automatically to clear the table, and was rewarded with a wan smile. Tom shot him a dirty look and recited, "May I be excused please and go out and play?"

Mrs. Robicheaux lifted a hand as if to restrain him, and hesitated. "Don't go far, Tom. Remember to check in."

"I will." The boy pushed himself back from the table and ran for the door, passing the suitcases as if he never even noticed them.

Sam continued to clear the table, trying hard not to let the plates and silver make a noise. After a while the woman sitting at the table got up and went back down the hall toward the bedrooms.

It was about time, Sam thought, for Al to show up. Maybe the Observer could tell him what to do next. Not that it wasn't clear enough: boyhood on a farm that didn't have time for fancy things like

17

dishwashers was excellent preparation for doing the evening dishes.

It was quiet in the apartment now. The only sounds were those of water, of a squeezed sponge, of his own—of Missy's own—feet as he stepped up and down from the metal stool Tom had tucked away in the corner. There was no television, no radio, no sounds of life from outside. It might have been spooky. Instead, it was comforting. It allowed him time to think, something to occupy his hands, and leisure to summon his patchwork of memories and formidable intelligence to the problem of who and where he was, and *why* he was where he was, this time.

And, perhaps, try to retrieve some more memories of his own youth. His idolized older brother Tom, the Vietnam vet, had . . . survived the war? Been killed? In one version of the past, Tom had died. But he thought he had a wisp of a memory of being the best man at his older brother's wedding, and if that were so, Tom must have lived. He remembered Leaping into a member of his brother's squad. He thought he saved him. Had he really? Did Tom die later?

He never knew when he changed things, if they stayed changed or not. Maybe that was why he kept on Leaping—to get the past nailed down the way it was supposed to be.

Supposed to be for what? So that Sam Beckett could get several doctorates, and design a hybrid, neurocell computer named Ziggy? Why did he do that? So that he could Leap into past lives and straighten things out so that he could get several doctorates, and. . . .

It was circular logic, and it offended him.

The only explanation he'd ever been halfway happy with was that the timeline that contained Sam Beckett wasn't as real as the ones he Leaped into and changed. He was making himself possible. Making some specific event possible, possibly something

18

besides the creation of Ziggy. Maybe he'd created Ziggy to correct something that had gone wrong in his own past. Tom's death, maybe?

If Tom was still alive, and Sam was still Leaping, it meant there was something else. And he couldn't remember what it might be, or even if there *was* anything at all.

Every time he Leaped, he was supposed to change something, put something "right." Fix a disaster, however minor or major, in someone's life. He had it down to a science now: He Leaped, shortly thereafter Al popped in with the link to Ziggy the computer and told him what Ziggy thought was supposed to change, he changed it, and he Leaped again. Except when Ziggy was wrong, of course, which happened more often than not.

But the change had to be made. He and Al had speculated that success had nothing to do with whether he Leaped or not, but if he wasn't supposed to change *something*, what was the point of Leaping at all? Or he might try and fail, and Whoever or Whatever was controlling the Leaps might send him somewhere Else to try again. If that was so, then there did indeed have to be a Plan, a Final Purpose to his dizzying journey through the last forty-some years of history. And every failure meant even more Leaps until whatever, in the greater scheme of things, finally got straightened out, and he could go back to being Sam Beckett in Sam Beckett's body and Sam Beckett's time. He wanted to go home.

At times like this, he was grateful for mundane chores like doing the dishes. Dirty silverware, at least, he could handle.

He finished drying the crystal water glasses and carried them out to place them carefully on the dining room table. He didn't want to take the chance of breaking one; they were lovely things, collecting prisms of light in the hand-cut sharp edges and throwing it back as rainbows on the drab walls. He wondered if they were heirlooms, and if so, why they were used for an ordinary dinner.

And that brought him back to the original set of standard questions. Who. When. Where. Why.

He had Leaped into the body of Missy Robicheaux, who was at best six years old. Missy had a brother, Tom, and a mother with a headache. She also had a father, a Major Robicheaux, who was mysteriously absent. So that was "who."

Judging from the cars, the time was the late Fifties. He saw nothing to contradict that estimate; he would check the newspapers and magazines on the coffee table so he could get a better idea of the date. He did think it rather strange that there was no television. He'd grown up with it, and its absence in this house felt like the gap when a tooth had been pulled—not painful, exactly, but an absence all out of proportion to its size. There had to be television; he could only Leap within his own lifetime.

He wondered whose Plan it really was, who decided that this time he needed to be six years old and female in order to fix whatever it was. God's? Fate's? Ziggy's? Sheer random chance? No; if it were chance, he wouldn't have to change anything in order to Leap again. There had to be some reason, some design to all this.

Most dreadful possibility of all, was it really his *own* design, and had he programmed Ziggy to do this to himself?

What was so terribly wrong with Sam Beckett's life that he would take it upon himself to change the universe? As far as he knew, or remembered, he wasn't an egomaniac to that scale, casually altering other people's lives to fit what *he* wanted. Was he?

He shivered, rejecting the idea.

"Somebody walking over your grave?"

It was Al at last, dressed in a natty red suit with a matching scarlet fedora and a paisley tie that shrieked against a black shirt. Sam nearly dropped a bone china plate in surprise. Not at the clothing—for Al, that was practically subdued—but at the suddenness of his appearance, out of nowhere. Which, in a sense, was a perfectly accurate description.

"Where have you been?" It was practically a ritual question by now.

"Working," Al said, with a self-righteous jab of his unlit cigar. "Trying to figure out why you're here. It isn't easy, when Verbeena won't even let me talk to the person in the Waiting Room." Al surveyed him carefully, from the tips of his Keds to the top of his braided head. "Aw, you're cute. But where'd you get the shiner?"

Sam sneaked a look over his shoulder before asking his next question. Sometimes he had a problem remembering that other people couldn't see Al, and his conversations with the Project Observer looked like conversations with thin air. But there was no one to see, this time, and judging from the silence down the hall, it didn't sound like Mrs. Robicheaux was coming out anytime soon.

So he shrugged, and responded, "Never mind about that. Why won't Verbeena let you talk to her? Do you mean you don't have any information?"

Al sighed. "Oh, I've got information. More information than I want. It's just not quite the *right* information that I want, if you follow me. But Verbeena won't let me in the Waiting Room because she's afraid our visitor is going to realize she's visiting in your body, and our headshrinker is afraid it will traumatize her little mind."

Why should Missy Robicheaux be any more traumatized than any other visitor? Sam started to ask. Then he looked down at the pink play-dress and reconsidered. He didn't often think about how his own body was being treated, hosting the minds or souls or awarenesses or whatever the hell it was, back in the Waiting Room; something to do with avoidance, he suspected. But if he closed his eyes and tried to imagine his body occupied by a six-year-old girl. . . . *His* bathroom problems didn't begin to cover it.

"So how did you get information, then?"

Al looked smug. This was an expression Sam had long since learned to distrust.

"Well?" he demanded.

Al flourished the collection of colored cubes that linked him to Ziggy and made a great show of examining the data link. "As it turns out," he announced, "we got a name, and that name shows up in lots and lots of files ranging from the Department of Defense to the KGB. What used to be the KGB," he corrected himself. Old military habits were hard to break. "You're in the body of Missy Robicheaux, and it's Saturday, August fifth, 1961—"

"Why would Missy be in KGB files?" Sam interrupted.

Al favored him with a glare. "*As* I was saying. Missy is the daughter of Major Steven Robicheaux, currently assigned to USAFE Camp Lindsay, Wiesbaden, Germany. She's in KGB files because her daddy has some classified duties related to cargo planes, and the KGB wanted to know everything about U.S. military personnel and every member of their families in case they could use the information somehow. She's in DoD files because she's a dependent."

"How can it be 1961?" Sam was still back on Al's original statement. "There aren't any cars of that model on the street out there."

"Because," Al said, giving up his planned presentation with a sigh, "military personnel stationed in Europe didn't get the latest models. For one thing, they couldn't afford them. Unless they had family money, or got lucky at poker, or something," he amended, clearly remembering his own service days.

"I'm in Europe?" The second chunk of information had finally sunk in. "I've never Leaped to Europe before! Al, that's fantastic!"

"To be exact, you're in Hainerberg, an Air Force military housing project near Wiesbaden, the Federal Republic of Germany. *And*—" he cocked a shaggy eyebrow at Sam, who took the warning not to interrupt any more—"in one more week, the Russians are going to start building the Berlin Wall."

CHAPTER

THREE

Office of Civilian Personnel
7100 HQ SUPPORT WING
Wiesbaden Military Post 22 May 1952:

"All hired help are required to have the following prior to employment: an identity card station political clearance; registration with the German police when recruited from another locality; physical examination and immunization by military post surgeons; social insurance card; and a wage tax card. . . ."

"The Berlin Wall? You aren't suggesting I'm here to stop the Wall?" Sam nearly fell off the step stool in shock.

"No, of course not." Al jabbed at the handlink and frowned. "At least, we don't think so . . . No, it's way too late to stop the Wall. The East Germans are leaving by the thousands, every day, and the Russians—yeah. They just forbade ministers to go to an interfaith conference in Berlin. Nope, Missy isn't going to stop the Wall."

"So," Sam said with exaggerated patience, "what *am* I here to do? Something for Missy?"

25

Al was faintly embarrassed. "Well, actually, as a matter of fact—"

"Let me guess. You don't know." Sam snapped a dish towel next to where Al would have been standing, if Al, instead of his hologrammatic image, had actually been standing there. "I thought you said you had all these files on her?"

Al crunched the cigar between his teeth. "Well. Sort of. We have the files on her father; he never got promoted past major. He's still alive. Her mother, let's see—" The data stream was fragmented and hard to read; he slapped the handlink and the jumble fell back into words. "Her mother dies in 1989. Her brother has a perfectly ordinary career as an electrical engineer, gets married, has a couple of kids."

"And Missy?"

Al cocked an eye at him. It was unsettling—with one part of his mind, the part linked through Ziggy, he could see Dr. Samuel Beckett. With another, he could see a little girl giving him a mutinous stare, lower lip stuck out, wisps of hair escaping from long braids. Sam was going to have to learn how to braid hair in this one. Al smothered a smile.

"Missy stays single. Gets a doctorate in psychology—now that's interesting, wonder if it's because of her childhood? Seems to be perfectly happy." He shook his head. "I don't know if having you Leap into her childhood's going to change that."

"So what happened to Missy in August of 1961?"

Al took a deep breath and shrugged. "Nothing, so far as we can tell." The datalink flickered. "Oh, wait. No. She broke her arm."

Sam's—or Missy's—jaw dropped. "She *broke her arm*? Are you telling me I Leaped here to keep a six-year-old from getting a broken arm? Is Ziggy sure about that? What happens, it doesn't get set right?"

The datalink cubes glowed in some sequence that made sense only to the computer. Al squinted at the screen. "Er, no. It doesn't seem to make any difference. Ziggy says there's only a sixty-two-percent chance that you're here to keep her from getting her arm broken."

"And that's all you've got? How does it happen?"

"That's all we've got right now," Al corrected him. "And we don't know how it happened. That part was never recorded anywhere, not even in the hospital records. Ziggy can't access what was never written down, you know. He can't read minds." Except maybe yours and mine, he did not add. He wasn't sure about that. The links, Ziggy's chips, were made from his nerve tissue and Sam's, after all—that was why he was the Observer, why he could always find Sam, eventually, no matter where in time he landed.

"Well, can't you ask her?"

"Ask who what?"

Sam spun around to see Missy's mother standing in the doorway. "Ah—"

"Ask what? Who are you talking to?" The woman sounded angry.

Al decided that this would be a good time to do a fade and leave Sam to the inevitable explanations. He waggled his fingers good-bye and pushed the handlink control that opened the Door back into the Accelerator.

The Imaging Chamber of Project Quantum Leap looked the same as it always did, an octagonal blue-white room with glowing panels for walls. He was standing on a silver disk. Another floated over his head. He released a breath he didn't realize he was holding and said, "Ziggy?"

"Admiral Calavicci," a bodiless feminine voice acknowledged. "There are no changes apparent since you left."

This breath he did know he was holding. Sam's mucking around in time meant that things weren't particularly stable in the Project. Little things could be different. Every once in a while, major changes occurred. So far the changes had unchanged themselves, and no one but Ziggy, and Al, were in a position to realize that anything had ever been different. It did make personnel matters interesting from time to time, though.

"What time is it?" he asked as he started down the ramp into the Control Room.

"Eighteen hundred hours," the voice informed him. "Most of the staff are in the cafeteria."

There was, in fact, no one in the Control Room, not even a technician to work on the great table made of colored cubes, a larger version of the handlink, that took up most of the space in the middle of the room.

"Is there anybody with the . . . in the Waiting Room?"

"Only our visitor." Ziggy was miffed. The computer didn't like to be left alone.

Al paused, looked up at the ceiling. "She's by herself? Verbeena's gone to dinner too?"

"That's correct, Admiral." There was a pause while the computer correlated the exchange with its database on Al Calavicci's behavior, made projections, and added warily, "Dr. Beeks specifically forbade you to enter the Waiting Room during this Leap, Admiral."

"Oh, come on. I just want to ask a couple of questions. I wouldn't hurt her."

"Dr. Beeks is concerned about the possible psychic damage the child may experience if she remembers awakening in Dr. Beckett's body."

"Hey, if there was going to be any damage, it would have already been done, right? If she's awake, she's figured it out. And it wouldn't be *me* hurting her. Come on, Ziggy. Can *you* find the information we need? That Sam needs?"

"I am pursuing several avenues of investigation," the computer protested.

"But it would really help if we had some ideas, now wouldn't it?" Al had perfected wheedling over the course of five marriages.

Ziggy, though more immune than any of the wives—not being burdened with hormones—recognized bullheaded determination when it scanned it. "I assume you will require advance warning if Dr. Beeks returns from the evening meal."

"Bingo," Al crowed, and headed for the Waiting Room.

Like all the working areas in the core of the Project, the Waiting Room was basic white, shaded in blue by the indirect lighting. A hospital bed, the latest thing in medical technology, was placed in the middle of the room. Stairs against the far wall led to the observation room, where a technician usually sat, keeping an eye on lights and readouts. But this evening, there was no technician; the individual in the Waiting Room was not confined to the bed.

Al paused in the doorway, watching. The other occupant of the room was sitting on the far side of the bed, head down, apparently staring at the floor. A white lab suit stretched across broad shoulders. Brown hair, grown a little longer than usual, lay flat against the nape of the neck.

Al bit his lip. Every time he entered this room he wanted to call out the name that ought to go with the person sitting on the bed, and every time he had to make himself stop and look again.

The person on the bed stood up and turned around.

Al's eyes closed involuntarily in denial.

It was Sam Beckett: It was certainly Sam Beckett's body. It was a man in his early forties, tall, fit but not thickly muscled, hazel eyes open and honest, well-defined jaw perhaps a shade long, a stray lock of hair, startlingly white against the brown, hanging down over his left brow.

But Sam Beckett's body did not move with its accustomed grace; the turn was clumsy, and one hand stretched out to catch at the bedsheets to prevent a fall.

And Al, looking into those eyes, saw instead of Sam Beckett a little girl, six years old and terrified.

He found himself wondering whether this was such a good idea after all.

"Hi there," he said, holding out a hand.

Sam—Missy—edged away from him. It was obvious that she'd been told never to talk to strangers, and all she had seen for the last several hours were strangers—Verbeena and her staff. Even her own body was a stranger suddenly.

"My name is Al," Al said. "Dr. Beeks says your name is Missy. That's a pretty name." He dropped his arm and remained where he was, and the person across the bed from him relaxed minutely.

"I bet you think this is a pretty strange place," he went on. "Have you ever been in a place like this before?"

Missy shook Sam's head. No.

He'd phrased it wrong, Al realized. He needed a question that required an answer of more than Yes or No.

And then he realized that he had another string to his bow. "Missy, your Daddy is in the Air Force, isn't he? What rank is he?"

"Major," came the prompt response. Sam Beckett's vocal cords made it much deeper than Missy's own voice, but she was hearing it with Sam Beckett's ears and brain, and she didn't flinch at the tenor pitch.

"I used to be in the Navy," Al confided. "I was an Admiral."

Instant skepticism lit the wide eyes. Like any military brat, she knew rank, and the man in front of her didn't look like an Admiral. Admirals didn't wear red suits. Only Santa Claus wore a red suit.

"Look," Al said. "I'll show you my ID." He fished in his lapel pocket for his wallet and slid the card out. "See?"

He had to put it on the bed between them. Once he retreated a few steps, Missy picked it up and examined it, looking from the picture to Al and back again. Even at six, a military kid knew what an ID card looked like, but Al hoped she was too young to pick up the differences between the ones her parents showed every time they entered the PX and the ID cards issued in the late nineties. The Robicheaux cards, for instance, probably didn't use a hologrammic American flag to keep them from being duplicated.

She caught on to the flag, tilting the card back and forth to make it wave, but accepted it as one of those strange things the Navy did. Surrendering the card reluctantly, she looked at him with an entirely different attitude.

"Now, Missy, you want to get home, don't you?"

A shadow passed over her face, but she answered promptly enough. "Yes, sir."

"Okay. I need to ask you some questions, and I need you to tell me everything you can. Can you do that?"

"Yes, sir." She was obedient. Alert. Respectful. Al wondered how much hell she raised when she was on her own.

"Okay. Now, you live in Hain—" he stumbled.

"Hainerberg."

"Yes. That. Okay. With your mommy and your daddy and your brother, right?"

"And Marta."

"Marta?" Who the hell was Marta, and why hadn't Ziggy said something about her? "Tell me about Marta."

"Marta's our maid. She lives downstairs in the maids' quarters."

A muffled squawk from a speaker said that Ziggy had had second thoughts about supplementing this information, at least while Al was talking to Missy. Al made a mental note to have a long talk with the computer as soon as he was through with the child.

"What's Marta like?" This was a whole new avenue of information; Sam's Leap could have something to do with the previously unknown Marta.

"She's *old*. She makes roses out of butter when I cut it up."

Al closed his eyes and nodded. Of course. "Do you like Marta?"

"She doesn't speak very good English," Missy said thoughtfully. "She doesn't speak very good German either."

Al opened his mouth to ask another question, then closed it again. Not very good German either? "How do you know?"

"I asked Renate. She says she's a dee pee."

Now Al was getting really confused. "Renate's a . . . oh, a displaced person?" In Germany? Well, certainly, but in 1961? Wasn't that kind of late, sixteen years after the war?

"What?" Missy was getting confused too, and withdrawing as a result. She knew initials, but apparently didn't know what they stood for.

"A DP, honey. Renate is a DP? Who's Renate?"

"*No.*" Her voice was sharp with frustration, and she brushed against Sam's forehead, shifting the lock of white hair out of the way. "Renate's my *friend. Marta's* a DP."

"Oh." It wasn't much clearer. Al decided to shift gears. "Okay. Tell me about your daddy."

Suspicion flared again. "Can't."

"Why not?"

"It's a secret." She was backing away again.

Al stopped. He'd never had kids of his own, thank God, but he knew plenty of fellow officers who had. Some of those officers had been involved in a number of Top Secret assignments. He'd never thought too much about how those assignments would affect their families. He had the uneasy feeling he was seeing that effect right now: Missy, only six years old, had clearly been warned repeatedly about anyone asking questions about what her father did. She was looking around the room now seeking an avenue of escape.

"And you're really good at keeping secrets, aren't you, Missy?" he said, making sure she could hear the approval in his voice. "I'll bet your daddy is really proud of you."

"Where's my daddy?" she said.

It was a wail of utter heartbreak, a little girl's cry in the voice of his best friend, and Al Calavicci couldn't handle it. "It's okay, honey, honest," he muttered, retreating toward the exit. "We'll get you home soon, I promise. I *promise*." He closed the door behind himself with a sigh of relief.

Which turned to a choke at the sight of Dr. Beeks waiting, arms crossed, standing in the corridor like an avenging angel.

"Exactly *what* do you think you're doing, Admiral?" she snapped. "I placed a restriction on the Waiting Room for this Leap. Just what were you doing in there?"

"I was trying to find out something to help Sam," he said. From the look in Verbeena's eye, she thought it sounded as weak as he himself did. "I *am* the Observer, Verbeena, it's part of my job."

"Not this time, it isn't. I don't want that little girl to be traumatized—"

"What could I do to her that's worse than she's already been through, Leaping into Sam's body?" Al demanded. "What are you gonna do, Verbeena, fill her up with drugs and keep her unconscious until Sam stumbles over what he's supposed to do that will get her back where she belongs? Don't you think she's noticed the body she's in already? Just because you don't have any mirrors in there doesn't mean she hasn't looked at herself and noticed some things are *real* different!"

33

Verbeena Beeks slumped against the corridor wall, crossed her arms in front of herself defensively, and eyed the man. "Yes," she admitted cautiously. "I've been telling her she's having a dream, and nothing bad is happening to her, and when she wakes up she'll be in her real body again. But I don't know how long she's going to believe that. I *have* considered putting her under—with *hypnosis*," she said, raising one hand to forestall Al's outrage. "I think it might be best, this time." The glaring lights threw ugly blue highlights against her dark skin, making her look tired. Or perhaps it was just the job that made her tired.

"I should have done something about the Waiting Room before," she muttered. "Every time, I think, why didn't we dress up this place a little bit? Why does everything have to be blue and white? Some calico curtains, something in green, would be so nice—"

"Ten stories underground?" Al was completely lost. "Why would you want curtains underground?"

"Never mind, Al." She gave him a weary smile. "It's just displacement worrying. But I want you to promise not to go in there again, okay?"

Al took a deep breath. "Okay, I promise. But you have to promise to ask her any questions that we come up with. I'm not going to leave Sam hanging for lack of information."

Verbeena was nodding, accepting the bargain, when Ziggy's voice interrupted. "Admiral, we have new data."

Al and Verbeena looked up at the ceiling simultaneously. "We do?" Al said. "What is it?"

"Unlikely as it originally appeared," the computer said, "there is now a ninety-four-percent chance that Dr. Beckett has Leaped into the body of Missy Robicheaux to prevent World War Three from breaking out over the building of the Berlin Wall."

CHAPTER
FOUR

ISSUE OF FURNITURE FOR MAID ROOMS,
7112th Supply Squadron, Office of Base Accountable Officer:
. . . the following policy will govern the issue of furniture for Maid Rooms within the Wiesbaden Military Post. . . .
  c. Only the following items are authorized to meet minimum requirements:
  (1) one cot, folding, steel
      one mattress, cotton
      two blankets, wool
      one pillow, cotton or feather

"Prevent World War Three? Al, that's ridiculous. World War Three never happened. If it had, we wouldn't be here. There. In the future. I mean—" Sam shook his head, frustrated. Time travel played hell with the tenses. "If World War Three had happened, the world would have blown itself up. If the world had blown itself up, the Project would never have happened, and I wouldn't be here now.

"Besides, I never change big things in history. Only little ones. So what's the deal here?"

35

Al sighed. "Ziggy says that you must have Leaped back originally to change something else. But something you've done in the meantime has caused a change that will cause the big kablooie."

"And does Ziggy have the foggiest notion what that 'something' might be?" Sam said, sitting up in bed and hooking his arms around his knees. "What does Missy have to do with the Wall, anyway? It hasn't even been built yet."

Al nodded. "Nope. Not for another week. Meanwhile, you remember Leaping into Eddie Ellroy?"

Sam nodded. He thought he could remember Eddie, whose brother Mack built bomb shelters. It had been a profitable business, feeding on hysteria. "So?"

"You remember how tense things were? Berlin is one of the big reasons why. And that was in the *States*—this is *Germany*. Man, they had thousands, *thousands* of people leaving East Germany, all their scientists and skilled workers and good people. They even passed a law against it. Khrushchev was making public speeches that warned that the world would be a smoking ruin by the time they got through with us. Our own generals were advocating pulling civilians out of Europe."

"She's *six*—" Sam caught himself shouting and lowered his voice to a whisper with a glance at the bedroom door. "She's six years old, Al! How could anything she does possibly make a difference to international politics and the Wall?"

Al shrugged. "I'm just telling you what Ziggy tells me. It has something to do with her father."

"Her father isn't even *here*!"

"No," Al agreed, squinting at the handlink. The light by which he read the datascreen came from the Imaging Chamber in which he stood, forty-odd years in the future. "Her father's in Berlin, watching the Russians gear up. Somehow he gets permission for a quick visit home—probably a side trip, since he'd be going back and forth between bases a lot. He comes back Monday night, and then he leaves again. And somehow, you've changed things."

"You'd think whoever was responsible for this would have more sense," Sam muttered, staring through Al into the darkness.

Al refrained from pointing out the possibility that Sam himself was responsible, not only for Project Quantum Leap but for the Leap pattern itself— that was one of several theories bruited about by the Project members who actually knew what happened to their Director—and chewed ferociously on his ever-present, unlit cigar.

"Ziggy's got to be wrong," Sam announced at last. "The whole scenario makes no sense. It goes against everything we know about my Leaping."

Al considered the randomly appearing and reappearing holes in Sam's memory and said nothing about "everything *we* know."

"Unless," the Project Director went on, tilting a little girl's head so that her hair fell over her shoulder, and brushing it impatiently aside in almost the same movement, "there's something about her father coming back."

"Ziggy agrees," Al said, watching the colored cubes blink in coded rhythm.

"That's good of him," Sam answered, dripping sarcasm.

"Getting a little snarky here, are we? Didn't you get your nap this afternoon?"

Sam favored him with a glare that would fry glass. Al chortled, then looked back at the datascreen. "Uh-oh."

"*Now* what?"

"Ziggy says that you have to keep Missy's father from losing some papers? We can't tell—maybe he leaves them behind?"

"Where is Ziggy getting all this? From data in a timeline that doesn't exist?"

37

"It's speculation. But it's ninety-four percent certain speculation."

Sam heaved a sigh. "So what's 'uh-oh' about it? Can't I just get him to stay an extra day or something?"

Al's mouth twisted. "I can't figure out how Missy can keep her father from reporting for duty. It just wouldn't happen, Sam. But according to this, it's got to."

Sam stared at him, confused. "Sure it can happen. All I have to do is . . . well, if something happened to Missy, he'd stay, right?"

Al shook his head. "No, Sam. He'd let his wife handle it. *You've got to understand*: This is the United States Air Force, Europe. This is Germany. This is the Berlin Crisis, Part Two. Sabres are rattling on both sides. Khrushchev is threatening to sign a separate peace treaty with East Germany and cut off all supplies to Berlin. Nearly a thousand people a day are running for the border. General Maxwell Taylor is talking about nuclear war, Robert Kennedy is warning Russia not to push us too far, and John Kennedy is holding press conferences about mobilization and asking Congress to fund a defense buildup. There are Russian troops maneuvering less than two hundred miles from here. Major Steve Robicheaux is not going to leave his post for anything short of Missy's dying. And possibly not even then."

Sam opened his mouth and shut it again. "Oh."

"Oh," Al agreed.

After a moment Sam said, "Maybe that's why his wife is leaving him."

Al stared at him as if Sam were suddenly speaking Finnish. He opened and closed his mouth a few times, and then punched at the handlink. A moment later, he said, "Where the hell did you get *that* idea?"

"Go look by the front door," Sam advised.

Al raised an eyebrow and punched the handlink again, blinking into nothingness. A few moments later he popped back, considerable relief on his face. "Oh, *that*. You mean the suitcases."

Sam nodded.

"That's not Janie leaving her husband. That's standard operating procedure." When Sam looked blank, he elaborated. "I keep telling you, Sam. It's 1961—*August* 1961. For years, every military family in Europe has had packed suitcases sitting by the front door. If the alert goes, they'd have two hours to collect the kids, get in the car, and get the hell out of town. Evacuation preparedness. Although two hours . . ." he paused, shaking his head. "Two hours would have been too long. And there really wouldn't be any place to run. They knew it, too. They couldn't possibly outrun missiles launched from 200 miles away. But those were the orders."

Sam watched him, curious. "Were you stationed here then?"

"What? Oh, no, I was learning to fly Phantoms back then. I studied it, though. Some people say that losing face over Berlin was what led to the missiles in Cuba, the Missiles of October, but that's not true. They're already building the Cuban missile sites. I think Berlin was just one of the things they did to distract us." He had an expression on his face Sam had rarely seen before: abstracted, thoughtful, sad. The lights from the handlink flicked on and off in an irregular pattern, illuminating his face in pink—orange—green—blue. His voice was very soft. "World War III was so close. It would have been so easy for it to happen. The littlest thing could have set it off. In a way, the miracle was that it *didn't* happen."

It wasn't the Al Sam was used to, and he wasn't sure he liked it.

"Al. *Al!*"

Al blinked.

"What does all this have to do with a six-year-old girl?"

Al took a deep breath. "I don't know, Sam. But it has to have something to do with it, because Ziggy says that we're in Neverneverland. A sort of quantum physics Limbo, until it's settled."

"Would you mind explaining what you just said?"

"Me? You're the genius." Al shook his head. "I'm just repeating what Ziggy says. In the original history, the big kaboom kafizzled. Now we're going down a path where it kablasts. But if it does, then the Project never happens, so you never Leap back, and whatever you did to change history never happens, so the Project *does* happen, and you Leap back, and. . . ."

"Never mind. I'm afraid I'm beginning to understand you."

"Things went kaka," Al summarized. "Until we know which way to jump—or Leap—"

"Please. Things are bad enough as it is. Don't you have any idea what changed things?"

"Sure. You did."

Sam threw a pillow at him. The pillow passed through and hit the top of the dresser, knocking a carousel music box to the floor.

"Missy!" The voice from the living room cracked almost as sharply as the carousel.

"Yes?" Sam answered, midway into picking up the pieces.

" 'Yes, Ma'am,' " Al warned him. The term of address was a title, as he used it.

Too late. The door came open so hard it hit the wall and bounced. The ceiling light popped on, blinding him. "Yes *what*?"

"Yes, Ma'am," Sam amended hastily.

"What are you doing in here?" Jane's gaze lit on the pink and gold rose shards of the carousel. "You broke it! That was my mother's!" She saw the pillow, too. "You were playing in here again, weren't you? I told you to go to sleep, didn't I? Didn't I! You stupid,

stupid, worthless brat! What did I tell you to do! What did I tell you!" Her voice was rising nearly to a shriek.

"Go to sleep," Sam whispered, backing away. But it was a small room, and he couldn't back far enough.

"Don't you touch him!" Al yelled helplessly, but it was too late. Jane's nails bit into Sam's shoulder, lifting him off his feet, and he rocked back with the force of her slap. "Shut up! Shut up, dammit! I don't want to hear it! You clean that up right now, and you get into that bed and I don't want to hear *one word* out of you till morning, do you hear me!"

"Don't say anything, Sam," Al warned. "Don't. Just pick up the pieces and put them on the dresser."

He waited until the talons digging into his shoulder loosened, and then bent down, face stinging, eyes stinging, to pick up all the pieces of the carousel and put them carefully on top of the dresser, lined up in a neat row. He gave Janie Robicheaux a wide berth as he moved around to the bed, got in, lay down and pulled the covers up to his chin, never looking away, never looking her in the eye. Her lips, white edged, were pressed into a thin line; her nostrils flared, her chest heaved. Everything about her said Suppressed Rage. With one part of his mind Sam wondered how much of it was an act. With another, he wished desperately that she would go away. He couldn't seem to stop shaking.

Al, standing next to the woman, was doing a fair rendition of fury himself. "You—you—you monster," he sputtered. "Hitting a little kid like that. How'd you like to pick on somebody your own size?"

Janie, of course, didn't hear him. She looked around the floor, searching for neglected bits and pieces; not finding any, she gave Sam one last glare and turned the light off, slamming the door behind herself.

"Some people shouldn't have kids," Al snarled, making a rude ethnic gesture to the closed door.

41

"I'll bet she's going back to hit the bottle some more. I hate a drunken female."

It took several deep breaths for Sam to bring the body's physiological reactions under control. "Maybe this is what I'm here for," he whispered. "To stop Missy from being hit."

"Well, World War Three *would* stop it," Al agreed, his attention jolted from the door back to Sam. "But it's a little more permanent than I'd like, personally. I'd rather you took care of the end of the world first, if you don't mind."

"A six-year-old child cannot stop a nuclear war," Sam said through clenched teeth.

"I didn't think she could start one, either, but it looks like that's what happened. Will happen. Might happen. . . ." Al gave up, frustrated.

Sam threw himself back against the mattress, reaching back for a post of the headboard. Missy's arm was too short. He had to scoot back up toward the pillow, and by that time no longer needed something to hold on to. He laced his fingers beneath his head instead. "I haven't done anything," he said thoughtfully, no longer protesting against the idea. "So maybe it's something that Missy did, or would have done, that I didn't do, or wouldn't do."

Al floated closer, punching at the handlink. "Ziggy says that there isn't any data, but logic says there's a fifty-fifty chance that you're right."

Sam rolled his eyes. "No. Really? Maybe you ought to go back and talk to Missy some more and *get* the data."

"I can't do that," Al answered without thinking. Then he saw the look on Sam's face, and rephrased. "Dr. Beeks won't let me do that."

"Fine by me." Sam raised and dropped his shoulders in a horizontal shrug. "I'm not the one who says the fate of the world depends on it. I'll just try to figure out a way to make Missy's mother stop hitting her."

Nonplussed, Al tightened his lips and looked from Sam to the handlink and back again. Sam was staring at the ceiling. Al nodded once, sharply, and punched in the recall. The Door opened behind him. He stepped into the opening and took one last look over his shoulder.

"Try to give the fate of the world some thought while you're at it, okay?" he said, and the Door snapped into nothingness, taking the Observer with it.

CHAPTER
FIVE

6. NONCOMBATANTS—DEFINED: The following personnel are considered noncombatants under the provisions of this plan:

    a. Dependents of members of the US Armed Forces, of US Government employees and of authorized Allied Nationals.

    b. US citizens and Allied personnel employed by the US government.

BY ORDER OF THE COMMANDER:

Missy Robicheaux sat on the edge of the bed and swung Sam Beckett's feet back and forth, back and forth, fascinated.

So this was what it was like to be a grownup. The beds got smaller.

She took a deep breath and looked around. There was a lady in the little room at the top of the stairs. She saw Missy looking and waved. Missy waved back, hesitantly, and then rubbed her hands together. They were so *big*, and yet they felt like they were just the right size.

This must be what Goldilocks felt like when she was eating all that porridge, Missy thought. Though she had always suspected that Goldilocks called

Baby Bear's porridge "just right" because she'd got so full eating Papa Bear's and Mama Bear's. These were Papa Bear hands, but they felt like her own, littler hands did. The sheets on the bed felt the same, no matter what size her hands were. If her swinging heels hit the bed frame, it still hurt.

It was a boy's body. She knew that. Her brother Tom showed her once how boys looked different. But when she needed to go to the little girls' room, it felt just about the same. She could aim better, though. That was interesting. She played with that for a while, and then she didn't need to go any more and the nurse lady came in and wanted her to take a pill. She didn't want to, though. Mommy took pills a lot. So they gave her a puzzle book instead. That was fun too.

The lady up in the little room was talking to a knob on a stick, sneaking looks at Missy when she thought Missy wasn't watching. The lady was probably talking about her, Missy deduced.

She wondered if in her dream she was going to have to stay in this body. She hoped not. She wished the dream people would tell her things. The lady in the little room, and the Negro lady in the white coat, didn't act like they wanted to tell her anything. It was probably a secret, like the stuff Daddy did. Sometimes Daddy talked to Mom about things, but he wouldn't tell her or Tom. Tom acted like he knew lots of things, but it probably wasn't true. Tom fibbed a lot.

The Negro lady in the white coat was a doctor, Missy thought, even though she'd never seen a Negro doctor before. She said her name was "Dr. Beeks." Like a bird's beak. Missy had never seen a lady doctor either. She didn't give shots, though, so maybe she wasn't a doctor at all. She asked lots and lots and *lots* of questions, and sometimes she stuck things on Missy's head and there were wires and a machine that lit up. Her hair was shorter than it

46

used to be. She reached up to feel and the lady in the little room started talking to the stick again. Missy waited. Sometimes things happened when the lady talked to the stick. Sometimes they didn't, but it was fun to watch. Nothing happened this time, though, so Missy just kept on watching her to see what she would do next.

That lady had dark hair and dark eyes, like Marta, but she wasn't fat like Marta. Missy wanted to go up into the little room and look around, see if maybe the lady put everything away the way Marta did. Dr. Beeks wanted to know if Missy was going to make her bed, but that was what Marta did.

The room was all white. The walls were white, the floor was white, the sheets on the bed were white. It hurt her eyes. She had to squeeze her eyes shut. The lady must have talked into the little stick again, because when she opened her eyes back up the light was different and her eyes didn't hurt so much any more.

She wanted to go out and play, but they wouldn't let her. She never saw anybody except Dr. Beeks and the lady she didn't know and once, a man who said he was an Admiral. He asked questions about Daddy, and Daddy said that she should never, never answer questions about what he did. She thought the man might have been an Admiral, even if he dressed funny. Sometimes Daddy didn't wear his uniform too, but he never wore clothes like that. But Admirals were Navy, and Daddy said the Navy did funny things, so maybe they had funny civvie clothes.

Dr. Beeks asked her once about Mommy. She didn't want to talk about Mommy, even though Mommy didn't do secrets. Missy thought Mommy might be mad because she was gone so long, but Dr. Beeks said it would be okay, Mommy knew where she was. Missy hoped that was right. She didn't like it when Mommy got mad.

Mommy hit.

• • •

Jane Robicheaux sat in her living room, paging through a fashion magazine without really seeing the words and pictures. It was something to do while waiting for the news. The upper right-hand door of the cabinet was open wide, revealing the combination radio and phonograph built in. A symphony was just finishing, and the announcer was rattling on in guttural German.

She should have gone to the bridge party tonight. She needed to make an appearance. But it was Marta's night off, which gave her a reasonable excuse. She didn't really want to deal with those other women who were always so perfectly turned out, so sure of themselves, who had such perfect children. None of them seemed to listen to the news.

She closed the magazine, impatiently, and tossed it back on the coffee table next to a copy of the *Stars and Stripes* that Missy had been play-reading. She'd gotten really absorbed in it, too. Jane's lips curved fondly. She had quite an imagination, did Missy—pretending she could really read, talking to imaginary friends. She supposed a singleton child needed that sort of thing. Missy was artistic, too. Like her mother and her aunt had been. Jane's face changed as she thought about all the plans she and Jeanne had had, before she married. She and Jeanne had shared their dreams and their art.

Of course, Missy was also clumsy, stubborn, impertinent, and talked back. She and Jeanne had never done that.

The telephone rang, and she jumped and clutched at it. It took a moment of strict discipline to wait for the second double ring.

"Hello?" There was a small pause, and then, with a delighted shriek, "Mother! Oh my goodness! Oh! How wonderful for you to—Mother? Is something wrong?"

There was another pause. "Jeanne? Jeanne? Oh, Mother, no—no . . ."

48

The voice on the other end was broken, too. "It was a terrible wreck, Janie, just awful, she was all broken—"

Jane Robicheaux doubled over, sobbing.

"—we know you can't just come back any old time, but she's your twin, honey, the funeral is on Wednesday—"

She cried again, and the handset fell, and she curled into a ball, howling to herself, wanting oblivion, wanting a bottle. . . .

5. **ITEMS FOR ASSEMBLY:**

a. The following listed items should be on hand in each family unit and plans made for their rapid assembly in the event of an emergency:

(1) Warm clothing including raincoats or substitute. Female personnel should wear slacks.

(2) Two (2) blankets per person.

(3) One (1) small handbag per person, containing a change of clothing, toilet articles, important family documents, etc.

(4) Individual identification, such as AGO cards, Passports, ID cards or Tags, etc.

(5) Military Payment Certificates and/or other negotiable dollars instruments (all on hand at time of alert).

(6) Inventory of household goods and personal effects.

(7) Two (2) days' supply of non-perishable packaged food stuffs, also canned milk for children.

(8) Suitable water containers to provide one (1) quart capacity per person.

(9) Automobiles with valid certificates of registration and title.

(10) A minimum of seven (7) gallons (or tank one-half full) of gasoline will be kept in the tank or otherwise immediately available at all times.

(11) One (1) first-aid kit, commercial or home made equivalent per automobile.

CHAPTER
SIX

" . . . 2900 East German refugees poured into West Berlin today in a desperate effort to escape before the Communists block air, sea, and land routes to the city. . . ."

Sam woke the next morning to the sound of a vacuum cleaner next to the bed, and opened his eyes to see a large, square-shaped woman with small, very dark eyes and equally dark hair leaning over the bed. She was wearing a worn, badly made navy blue cotton dress.

The woman said something in a language Sam didn't understand. But her impatient gesture was clear enough, and he jumped out of bed and ran for the bathroom. The bruise on his face was turning yellow around the edges.

By the time he returned the woman was smoothing down the newly made bed, grunting softly as she straightened up. She glared at Sam and spoke again, this time in English. "You sleep all day? Lazy girl! Get dressed! Breakfast waiting!"

Sam gulped and opened the dresser, trying to act both as if he knew what he was doing and as if it didn't bother him to have the woman watch as he shed the pajamas and got dressed. Missy had a drawer full of underwear, another one full of shorts and shirts. He didn't think she would be wearing a dress. He looked at the large woman for confirmation of his choice. Her expression was blank, neither approving nor disapproving. It must be all right, he decided.

He was wrong, as he discovered when he showed up at the breakfast table. Tom was wearing a blue suit, white shirt and a tie, his hair neatly slicked back. Mrs. Robicheaux was wearing a brightly flowered dress. There was nothing on the breakfast table but glasses of water.

"Am I to understand," Mrs. Robicheaux said with glacial calm, "that you are not going to go to Mass with us today?"

Sam winced. It was Sunday, August 6. He wished Al had been there to remind him. "I forgot."

"Do you want God to forget *you*?"

"No, ma'am." He turned and ran for the bedroom again. The large woman looked at him again and sniffed, coiling up the cord to the vacuum and dragging it along behind her to the next bedroom. Missy's parents', Sam thought.

He had no idea when Mass was supposed to begin, but probably soon, based on Tom's appearance. Remembering himself as a ten-year-old, he didn't think the boy would be able to preserve that pristine sharpness for very long.

He would deal with how to behave when he got there. With luck, Al would show up to coach him through the Mass; he seemed to recall that the Tridentine Mass, before Vatican II, was pretty complicated, with lots of kneeling and standing and sitting. At least, it was complicated from the point of view of a midwestern Protestant farm boy. On the other hand, it would be in Latin, and he could handle Latin. He'd translated Suetonius for fun as an undergraduate.

54

Come to think of it, that probably wouldn't help much after all. He doubted they would be spending much time on Caligula.

The selections in the closet were limited: four dresses, all with frills and ruffles. A scuffed pair of white patent leather shoes neatly aligned on the floor suggested themselves by their very uniqueness. He closed his eyes, trying to remember how Katie dressed for church on Sunday. Pink. There was lots of pink involved.

Missy didn't lean to pink, apparently, despite yesterday's play dress. There was, however, a sunny yellow dress in a light fabric. He slid it over his head and struggled with buttons and a bow that tied behind his back, found a pair of socks, slipped on the shoes, and ran back for the dining room.

A look of great pain crossed Janie Robicheaux's face. "Go have Marta do your hair," she said. "You have five minutes." She took an elaborate look at her watch.

He imagined that she meant it. He went looking for Marta. At least he now had a name to go with the large woman.

The door to the master bedroom was closed. He opened it without knocking. "Marta?"

Marta was on her hands and knees on the other side of the queen-size bed, and her head popped up in response to his call. "What?"

"Could you help me with my hair, please?" Sam said. It was, he realized, sticking out in all directions, half-loosed from the rubber bands confining the pigtails. It hadn't even occurred to him to check his hair before going out before. He had to remind himself that he was a little girl now. At least, occupying the body of a little girl. A little girl with long hair, unfortunately.

The room was dark, dark from the black cherry furniture and the graying carpet and walls washed to pale streaks. On the tall dresser was a black-and-

55

white photograph of Jane Robicheaux, her pale face accentuated by dark lipstick, her hair done up in a coronal braid; facing it was a portrait of a man in Air Force uniform, lean and handsome, peering hawk-like from under the visor of his hat. Another framed photograph on the wall showed Jane and another woman, her mirror image, in identical high school prom formals, seated at an angle to each other as if to emphasize their resemblance. Another photograph showed Tom and Missy, painfully scrubbed and not happy about having their picture taken.

Marta had to grasp the edge of the dresser to pull herself up, knocking the picture of Major Robicheaux out of alignment.

"I need my hair done," Sam repeated.

"Not supposed to be here," Marta said. "Go to your room."

"Missy! Three minutes!" came the warning echoing down the hall.

Heaving a vast sigh, Marta herded Sam back into Missy's bedroom and pulled the rubber band off, catching a few strands as she did so. Sam smothered a yelp. Marta's thick fingers were efficient but gentle, taking a bristle brush and sweeping it through Missy's long brown hair, twisting it into neat precise braids.

She was almost finished when she paused. Her gaze met Sam's in the miniature dresser's mirror, and shifted to the door. Her hands rested lightly on Sam's head as she thought, and decided, and started over yet again.

"Missy!"

"Coming!"

Marta was creating a smooth, even French braid, tight against Missy's scalp. She had just completed tucking in the final wisps when Mrs. Robicheaux appeared in the doorway. "Are you ready?"

"Yes, ma'am." Marta was still standing behind him, and he was unable to duck away from the hand

56

that grasped his shoulder and pulled him forward and around.

"I suppose that will do." Jane Robicheaux sounded almost disappointed. "Get downstairs." Without acknowledging the other woman, she turned and left, forcing Sam with her through the apartment, past the waiting suitcases and out the front door.

It was Sam's first time outside. The large numeral 5 on the apartment door was matched by a 6 on the door opposite on the small landing. He tried unsuccessfully to catch a glimpse of what was upstairs as he was hustled down the stairs between Mrs. Robicheaux and Tom.

Tom led the way to a robins'-egg blue Chevrolet station wagon, scrambling into the back seat. From his body language, Sam gathered that Missy shared the back seat with her brother. He also gathered that Tom regarded this with a mixture of glee and disgust.

It didn't matter. He looked out the window with intense curiosity. He thought he remembered visiting Germany at some time or another, but his memory was as always uncertain, and in any case he had never had the chance to see it like this. It was hot and humid, a haze of water vapor on the horizon, and once out of the American housing area the surviving trees were tall and lush and green. Elegant old carved-stone buildings alternated with open spaces, almost like miniature parks that hadn't quite matured yet, and ugly new construction with signs in German. After a few blocks he figured out that the miniature parks had been places once occupied by elegant buildings too, bombed into rubble during the war. The ruins had been tidied away. Almost every house had window boxes riotous with flowers. The streets and the sidewalks were scrupulously neat.

The people along the way stared at the station wagon as it went by. He caught glimpses of people glancing at one another as they passed. He tried waving to the children, dressed in white aprons or gray shorts and shirts. No one responded. Tom laughed at him and thumbed his nose out the window. Jane caught sight of this in the rearview mirror.

"Tom! Stop that this instant!"

Tom stuck out his tongue at the back of his mother's head, but subsided. The station wagon pulled into the parking lot of the American Chapel, a new building tucked between older ones like an upstart relative or an unwanted visitor, and nosed into one of the last parking places. They exchanged greetings with other worshipers as they approached the front door; Sam paused a moment to scan the sign in front, which listed services for Catholics, Protestants, and Jews.

As he turned in response to Jane's edgy command, he caught the eye of another woman who was staring at him curiously. He thought for a moment that the woman actually saw *him*, until he overheard her asking Jane about "Missy's poor little eye."

Jane shook her head. "I really don't know what I'm going to do with that child," she said. "She was running in the apartment and tripped and hit the edge of the coffee table. It scared me to death; I thought she was going to lose the eye! But it's just a bruise, and she'll be fine. Children bounce back so quickly, thank God." Sam looked up at her, marveling. He had never heard anyone lie quite so fluently before.

Evidently neither had the other woman. She smiled, a patently false smile that said, "I don't believe you for a minute, dear, but I'm not going to show the bad manners to dispute you," and nodded and moved away. Tom came over and tried to punch Sam in the arm. Sam dodged, keeping Jane between Tom and himself as they entered the chapel.

There was no stained glass, and the pews and

the kneelers were removable; a table flanked by a pair of lecterns at the front of the room served as an altar. It didn't feel like a church at all.

"You put your fingers in the water and you cross yourself," a voice said in Sam's ear as they paused at the entrance to the sanctuary.

"Al! Where have you—"

"Shhhh," Al said, in chorus with Jane, who reached for a braid to pull and found her hand sliding off the French braid instead. Al's voice was uncharacteristically low pitched as he continued, "You can't talk here. Do what I do."

Al had to repeat the gesture twice, in slow motion, for Sam to catch what he was doing out of the corner of his eye. But Tom and Jane and everyone else who came in was doing it too, dipping the tips of their fingers into the water in a white marble half-cup fixed to the wall. They touched their wet fingertips to forehead, chest, and left and right shoulders in order, a smooth flowing gesture that Sam imitated awkwardly. He knit his brows to Al in interrogation, was startled when Al shook his head.

Al didn't have his cigar, Sam noticed. And he was dressed in a relatively conservative striped gray-and-white shirt and matching silvery gray suit.

Al was actually attending the Mass, he realized shortly. He watched, fascinated, as his best friend made the responses and stood and knelt with the rest of the congregation. He couldn't sit without sitting on someone; the hologram hovered in the aisle between the rows of pews.

Sometime after an incomprehensible sermon, people began standing and filing out of the pews, advancing in orderly twin rows down to the altar. Jane and Tom stood too. Sam made as if to go after them, and Al punched in a query, wincing as the handlink squealed. The sound was audible only to Sam and Al, but Al shushed the little machine anyway. "You haven't had First

59

Communion yet," he whispered. "Stay where you are."

Sam wasn't exactly clear about what First Communion was, but he remained where he was. Eventually Jane and Tom filed back into the pew, knelt and bowed their heads. Tom looked angelic. Jane looked weary.

Al floated past Jane and leaned over to whisper in Sam's ear as the rest of the congregation moved up to the altar, spread along the rail, received Communion, and marched back to their pews. "Ziggy says that Major Robicheaux will be back tomorrow evening—Monday—because the chaplain called him; she's had a death in the family. He's going to be bringing with him some plans for the mobilization of American forces. The number of East Germans leaving has gone through the roof, and the Russians are mobilizing tanks on the other side of the border. Ziggy says the Russians somehow get a look at the plans—"

"Soviets," Sam hissed. "It wasn't the Russians, it was the Soviets."

Jane nudged him sharply with an elbow.

Al sighed and continued, his voice still low. "As far as anybody in the here and now is concerned, Sam, it's the Russians. It's Khrushchev. Don't interrupt, you're in church. Now, the Russians get a look at the plans and decide it means the Americans are going to do a preemptive strike. So they preempt our preemptive strike, and—"

"The world goes boom," Sam finished.

"*Ite, missa est*," the priest intoned.

Go, the Mass is ended, Sam translated automatically. The congregation rose and filed out; Jane collected her two and waited in the pew until almost everyone was gone. Then she said, speaking very softly, "You ought to know that your Aunt Jeanne died in a car wreck yesterday. Your Gramma called me to let me know. We're going to ask Father Jacobs

60

to say a Mass for her, because we can't go back for the funeral."

"Who's Aunt Jeanne?" Sam asked, without thinking.

Jane's face crumbled, and she fumbled for a handkerchief.

"Her twin sister, Sam," Al supplied. "Boy, you put your foot into it."

"I'm sorry," he said helplessly. But Jane was still weeping, and Tom looked at him with contempt.

"You don't even remember her," Tom said. "You were too little. She's Mom's sister. She looks just like Mom."

Sam bit his lip. And Jane wept.

CHAPTER
SEVEN

"Khrushchev claimed today that it was 'a fairy tale' that the West would fight to preserve Berlin, and that 'hundreds of millions will die in a nuclear holocaust . . . ' "

Sam returned to the Robicheaux apartment with Jane and Tom to find a full meal laid out on the dining room table. Sunday brunch was a tradition in the Robicheaux household. Sam noticed in bemusement that the butter came in squares, and had been carved into very realistic-looking yellow roses. "Marta," Al advised.

Sam ate his bread dry rather than spoil the cholesterol creation. Tom had no such compunction, mashing a rose flat with the butter knife and taking a large swipe out of it. The three of them ate in silence, the only noise the sound of silver against china. Al stood by, examining the handlink and bouncing back and forth impatiently. Sam bolted the last of his French toast, eager to get away from the gray depression surrounding the meal. "Ask to be excused," Al prompted.

"May I please be excused?" It reminded Sam of his own childhood, the manners his parents had instilled in him. But his mother had never given him the icy glance that Jane Robicheaux bestowed upon her daughter. He found himself checking over his plate to make sure it was empty, his knife and fork to make sure they were properly aligned across the small pool of syrup.

"Go change your clothes," she said at last. Sam pushed away from the table. "Tom, I didn't say you could go anywhere," he heard her say behind him to Missy's brother.

"Don't wear the shorts," Al advised him as he peeled off the yellow dress and hung it back up.

"Why not?" Sam said, pausing as he held up the brief khaki clothes.

"The Army decided shorts were in bad taste last month, and issued an order that women couldn't wear them. Bermudas are okay, though."

"You're kidding, aren't you?"

"What? No, of course not. No shorts, no bikinis on the wives, daughters, or civilian employees of U.S. military personnel. Didn't apply to the Air Force, of course, but they pretty much adopted it too. Couldn't have the Army being more moral than the Air Force." Al, a Navy man himself, shook his head. "Bermuda shorts were okay, though. See if she's got any of those."

Sam shook his head, put away the khaki shorts and burrowed deeper in the dresser. "Are these okay?" he said, holding up a pair of Bermudas and the orange-and-yellow blouse he had changed out of earlier. Even he could see that they didn't match.

Al's mouth twisted. "Well, for a six-year-old, I suppose so. Yeah, go ahead."

Sam dressed himself. "Okay," he asked, pulling the same blouse over his head, "how do the plans disappear? Marta?"

Al had the look of a man whose surprise had been spoiled. "How'd you know?"

Sam shrugged. "It's only the *body* of a six-year-old, remember? Besides, who else could it be? She's from the East, isn't she?"

Al nodded, studying the handlink. "No. Yes. Well, she's from the German-Polish-Russian-your-guess-is-as-good-as-mine border area, so it's kind of hard to tell. She's definitely a displaced person. She's also an agent of the East German intelligence services, planted on the family. I wonder how many of the maids were actually agents? They were supposed to be cleared."

"I imagine not as many as the Soviets would've liked, given the tensions of the times. Maids would be in an excellent position to do damage if people got careless."

Al nodded, giving a low whistle as he read the datascreen. "Yeah, yeah. That's it. Ziggy says Tom Robicheaux has the plans in his briefcase and Marta reads them, passes them along. Ka-blooie."

"So all I have to do is tell the Major that the maid is a spy, and it'll all be over." Sam looked into space, remembering the look in Marta's dark eyes when she changed her mind and got rid of the convenient handles Missy's braids made. He closed his eyes and took a breath. "It makes sense."

"But you don't like it." Al's mouth twisted. "You've got another one of those damned gut feelings again, don't you." He looked at the handlink. "Sam, World War Three is receding. How can you argue with that?"

Sam leaned back, staring at the ceiling. "I can't argue with it. It just seems like a bigger thing than I usually handle, you know. I'm only one person. Things as big as nuclear wars take more than one person to start, and more than one person to prevent."

"Things as big as nuclear wars," Al said firmly, "take the cumulative actions of individuals to start. And the cumulative action of individuals to stop.

One person can stop the cumulation."

Sam dropped his head and stared at the dapper figure in silver gray. "That's pretty profound, coming from you."

"It's the people I hang out with," Al growled. "Don't make a big deal out of it."

"I wasn't planning to." Sam paused. "Wait a minute. You said it was 'receding.'"

"Thirty-seven percent," Al agreed. He frowned at the handlink, slapped it in frustration. "It's stuck. It's not moving any more."

Sam waited.

"It won't drop any more. I can't figure it out."

"Maybe there's a chance I don't tell him?"

Al shook his head, slowly. "I can't imagine you not telling him." He looked over at Sam, seeing an earnest little child with smoothly braided brown hair and dark blue eyes, porcelain skin, and a rosebud mouth; seeing a six-foot-tall man with brown eyes and brown hair, with a single streak of white at his left temple. Since the process that combined nerve cells with computer chips and created Ziggy, Al would know Sam anywhere, anywhen. He knew Sam better than anybody.

And he literally couldn't imagine Sam not telling the Major about his housemaid.

But he looked at Sam again, and saw a six-year-old girl, and he wondered if the Major would bother to listen.

Tina Martinez-O'Farrell placed cotton between her toes, the tip of her tongue between her teeth, and a tiny brush into a tiny bottle. The brush came out dripping red. She dabbed at the nail of the large toe on her left foot, cocked her head to consider the effect.

It was, like, pretty.

Each toe received the same treatment in turn.

Now came the hard part. If the Project just wasn't so far away from everything, she'd have her quick-dry spray and she wouldn't have to worry. But she kept forgetting to buy it, and they wouldn't keep it on hand, no matter how much she explained to Supply that she really *needed* it. They kept telling her that it wasn't considered necessary for Project operations. Only necessary things were stocked by Supply.

Quick-dry wasn't necessary.

Neither was clam chowder, but they always had lots of *that* on hand. Nonieha told her in private it was because the Director *liked* clam chowder. Tina had said that *she* liked quick-dry spray, but Nonieha said that didn't count.

Stretching out one long leg, she splayed out her toes and gave them one last critical look. They'd do. She'd have to wait a little while longer before she did her other foot.

Her quarters in the depths of the Project were decorated in frills and ruffles and tiny prints, with lots of satin pillows flung around. She was dressed in old-fashioned pink baby-doll pajamas, and her red hair was up in huge rollers, and she looked like anything but an expert in computer architecture. Her voice was high and breathy and suffered from vocal pauses, except when she was presenting professional papers. She liked red toenail polish and self-lighted jewelry and lots of ruffles and satin pillows and really, really well designed computers. The Project was one of her very favorite places, even though she couldn't tell anybody about it, because it had Al and Gushie and the very best computer in the whole world. It used to have Sam Beckett, too, but Dr. Beckett was too involved with his work to notice her, even if—she rotated her foot in the air and decided the nails were dry enough to remove the cotton—she did use her very best perfume.

Still, if he ever came back from this Leaping thing, maybe he'd notice her. Probably not, and she certainly wouldn't want to hurt either Al or Gushie for the world, but it was fun to think about. He certainly was handsome, and he was smart, too. It wasn't easy to find a man as smart as she was. So Project Quantum Leap was probably the very best place that Tina Martinez-O'Farrell could possibly be.

But she *did* wish they'd stock quick-dry spray.

Meanwhile, she'd have to ask Ziggy who was on her calendar this evening.

Elsewhere in the living quarters of the Project, Dr. Verbeena Beeks leaned back from the large screen and rubbed her eyes wearily. The lighting in the office side of the room dimmed in sympathy.

"Next reference," she said.

The screen blinked. A moment later, when Verbeena still hadn't removed her hands from her eyes, Ziggy asked, "Do you require an analgesic, Doctor?"

Verbeena heaved a sigh. "No, thanks. Aspirin isn't going to help this time."

"There isn't anything in the literature about this particular subject, you know," the computer remarked. "I have one hundred forty-two more citations related to multiple personality syndrome, but that isn't the same thing at all."

"No, it isn't," she agreed. It used to be disconcerting to carry on a conversation with someone who not only wasn't there, but wasn't even a person. Computers weren't supposed to be capable of this kind of independent judgment. Some months after arriving at the Project to take the position of observing psychologist, she'd come to the conclusion that her primary patient was going to be a computer. And she'd never be able to publish.

She couldn't even write to her sister and tell her what was really going on. Anisha wrote her long letters asking her if she was still working with the famous Dr. Beckett, and she'd write back saying no, she was doing some disassociative reaction studies. Anisha would write back about her accounting firm and her husband and kids and wonder when they were going to get together for a vacation again—"Ver, you're always so *busy*!" And it was true, she *was* busy. Trying to figure out how much of Ziggy was Ziggy, how much was Sam Beckett, and if a computer could have had a childhood trauma.

She'd have to go visit Anisha soon. Really soon.

Glancing up at the wall, she felt her lips curve into a smile. She had pictures of her parents, of her sister and her sister's family, of their graduations and commencements and weddings. Verbeena had never missed having children of her own; 'Nisha's had always met her craving for young ones, and the scientists, engineers, technicians of the Project, even the ones older than herself, filled her need for older ones, her need to be needed.

But she *would* like to be able to publish again.

"Ziggy," she said at last, "what do *you* think about it?"

There was a long silence. Sam had programmed pauses into Ziggy's responses. Verbeena thought they probably signaled "You're not going to like this answer."

"I'm not sure I know what you mean," Ziggy responded. "Could you be more explicit, Doctor?"

Translation: "You're *really* not going to like this answer."

Verbeena crossed her legs, lotus-fashion, and swiveled around in her chair. "I mean, what do you think about Dr. Beckett's current Leap, Ziggy? I know you have an opinion."

"I don't have opinions, Doctor." Ziggy had a very human voice, and it was disconcerting to hear it coming from everywhere and nowhere at once. Verbeena had decided long since that for conversation purposes, Ziggy would be "present" at a point on the

69

ceiling, about two feet from the corner opposite the door.

She faced that point now and raised an eyebrow.

"I have hypotheses," the computer continued.

"Oh. I see. Well, tell me about your hypotheses." Another long pause.

"I think," the computer said, its voice remarkably hesitant, "that the net result of Dr. Beckett's Leaping is to move us outside of Time completely. So many things have been changed, so many possibilities extinguished and so many new futures created, that we represent the sum of all that is possible. But since not everything that is possible can coexist, we've been—shunted aside, if you will. In some sense, in order for us to exist at all, we have to have had existed. We wouldn't be where we are if we'd never existed. And yet this is self-evident."

The computer paused again, and Verbeena held her breath. She'd never heard Ziggy become quite so philosophical before. She recognized the trait from Sam Beckett's personality, but had never seen it quite so clearly expressed in his brain child.

"The course in which Dr. Beckett is currently engaged has a measurable chance of resulting in a global holocaust," Ziggy went on. "Yet we know this has not happened, because if it had, we wouldn't be here to consider the possibilities. That, in itself, decreases the probability to zero. Yet, it *might* happen. If it did, of course, we would all wink out of existence as if we had never happened."

Verbeena looked at the pictures of her family, and her lips tightened.

"In one sense, Dr. Beckett is independent of us, and the changes he makes are real changes. He could, therefore, end the world. Or prevent the world from ending." Ziggy was fretting now. The psychologist imagined she could hear the strain in its voice. "He—and I extrapolate we, though I'm not certain about this—exist independent of the original

70

history. He can change the past—any of the pasts—because none of them are really his own."

"I'm not sure I follow your reasoning," Verbeena said cautiously. The computer was beginning to sound like an obsessive-compulsive she had treated once as an intern. The patient had fixated on walking around a red chair and sitting in it. He did this for hours at a time. When interrupted, he became violent. He'd hold rational conversations as long as you let him walk around the chair, sit down, get up, walk around the chair, sit down, get up. . . .

"I'm not certain I understand them either," Ziggy admitted. "The whole concept of time travel is strictly science fictional. It doesn't really make sense at all."

Breakthrough! Verbeena thought, and then she considered that her current "patient" was several miles of flash memory and computing abilities created of melded silicon chips and human nerve cells, buried under empty acres of lava and caliche, and wondered who she was kidding. Sam Beckett had spent entirely too much time reading Asimov as a child, she decided.

"Is the world going to blow up or isn't it?" she demanded.

"I don't know." Now Ziggy was back to its old, petulant self, and Verbeena breathed a sigh of relief.

It was just as well she couldn't publish, she decided. Nobody would believe this anyway.

Sam could hear shouting coming from the dining room. Tom was arguing with his mother about going out again. She was telling him he couldn't go, that he had to stay in the apartment. He had to apologize to someone first. Tom was complaining that he never got to go anywhere or do anything, that he hated this place, and he was *leaving* and that was all there was to it. There was a sudden yelp of pain, and the

71

shouting stopped. Sam could hear footsteps coming down the hall, and fought the impulse to hide. He could hear a door open, and Mrs. Robicheaux say, "You stay in here until you learn proper manners, young man."

The door closed again, and the footsteps crossed the hall. Another door opened, and Sam relaxed. Mrs. Robicheaux was in her bedroom. Missy had evidently learned that the sound of her mother going into her bedroom and closing the door meant at least temporary safety; the relaxation was a learned reflex.

He thought about going out and doing the dishes and decided that he wouldn't. It might, after all, attract unwanted attention. So he stayed where he was, and when the door to Missy's room edged open a few minutes later, he greeted Tom without surprise. It was what his own older brother would have done, too, if he'd been sent to his room. Though Sam couldn't remember that ever having happened.

Tom was at least four years older than Missy, several inches taller and much heavier. Sam watched curiously as the boy, ignoring his sister, came over to the windowsill and picked up one of the toy horses, turning it over and over in his hands as if he had never seen it before. Tom put it down and picked up another, angling his body so that Missy could see what he was doing. Sam got the impression that he was waiting for Missy to protest, that his handling the toys was a means he used to torment his little sister. Since Sam wasn't his little sister and the toy horses meant nothing to him, he merely watched. Since the toys belonged to the little girl whose body he occupied, he promised himself that if Tom were to damage them in some way, he'd be in for a considerable surprise.

"I wish I could run away," Tom said at last, collapsing into a cross-legged heap on the floor. He was wearing a long-sleeved shirt with wide horizontal stripes in green and brown, brown pants, and tennis shoes. His hair was trimmed very short. He looked neat and clean, well fed, well cared for. "I wish I was an orphan," he said.

CHAPTER
EIGHT

. . . "no true military wife would admit worries to herself, or especially to her husband. It just isn't done."

Jane Robicheaux held her fingers to her temples as if doing so could prevent her pounding head from splitting open. The neighbors had heard her screaming at Tom, she was certain. And they'd heard Tom's cry of pain. *She* could hear Tom's cry of pain still, echoing in the empty living room.

She could still see his face, red with rage, shouting at her. She and Jeanne had never, *never* spoken to their parents the way Tom spoke to her.

Jeanne. A stifled wail echoed, twisted inside her. She took a quick breath, ignoring it, stifling it. She had to cope with her children now, not mourn—

She couldn't imagine speaking that way. But nothing she did seemed to affect him. She'd tried reasoning, and she'd tried ordering him to his room, and she'd tried spanking, and nothing seemed to work.

It was as if each time they moved, Tom got worse. As a baby, he'd been stubborn in Hawaii, when they were stationed at Hickam Field. At Wheelus he'd taken to refusing to answer her. In Washington he'd started talking back—at least there they'd been living among civilians. Now he was rude, disobedient, angry all the time. Snippy to a colonel's wife! Defying direct orders! She'd tried to explain it to his father, but Steve just looked at her and said, "Take care of it."

Steve didn't want his brother officers thinking he couldn't maintain order in his own family. And Jane could remember vividly the very first Officers' Wives luncheon she had attended, just a year after she and Steve were married, where the topic of conversation was a captain's wife who wore her skirts right at the knee and didn't leave cards when she visited. When she closed her eyes, she could still see the bright eyes, the shared thin knowing smiles, hear the clink of silver and glass and the well-bred amusement. She had felt, then, that any minute they were going to realize that she wasn't really one of them, and they'd turn on her and tear her to pieces too, and Steve's career along with her. Instead she'd smiled too, not quite sure about all the gaffes they chuckled over but chuckling too, just to be like them, just to look the same.

She'd tried to tell Steve, and Steve had looked at her again. It was the look that said, "Of course things are this way. Why do you want them any other way? What's wrong with you?"

Children out of line, wives acting inappropriately, did nothing to forward a man's career. Somehow, she had to find a way to keep Tom in line, or at least quiet, so people wouldn't talk about him.

Shuddering, she went into the kitchen and got out the bottle of gin. It tasted terrible; that was one of the ways, she thought, that you could control your drinking, one of the ways you knew you didn't really have a problem—you only drank things you hated, so you never really drank too much. She half filled a water glass and took a long swallow, shuddered and grimaced. After a moment the warmth began, and she could feel the large muscles begin to relax the least bit.

They weren't even supposed to be in Hainerberg, they were supposed to be in Crestview, where the senior officers lived. But Steve was on temporary duty in Berlin when the orders came, and she'd had a week to get the kids ready and have everything shipped from Washington to Europe. And when they got to Wiesbaden, there was no housing at all available, and they'd had to stay in a hotel. It wasn't her fault that the first halfway suitable place to become available was in a development that housed both officers and NCOs. She'd had to decide all by herself, not even talking it over with family.

But it meant that Steve was the highest-ranking officer in the building, and it meant that people watched him. Watched *her*. All the time. Steve hadn't said anything to her when he'd come in and found out what happened. He was always one to make the best of things. But still, he was disappointed; he'd wanted to be in Crestview. She could tell from the look in his eyes. Then he'd left again, and she'd had to get Tom into the American School in the middle of the year and find something for Missy to do.

Poor Missy. She'd just made friends in Washington, brought home a little girl from kindergarten, and then they'd moved again. Missy never complained. But it didn't seem right, somehow, for a little girl to give up her friend so willingly, as if friendship was one of those things that was temporary anyway. She was so quiet. Never any problem, really. She didn't have to think about Missy.

She had to think about Tom. Tom didn't understand that he couldn't just go wandering off. She had to know where he was every minute. She listened to the news on the radio every night, listened to Khrushchev's threats and the planes flying overhead, and prayed that the Russians wouldn't come; she woke up in the middle of the night, sweating, sure that the evacuation alert siren had gone off and she'd missed it, that everyone in Hainerberg had left, packed everything in their cars, and she and Tom and Missy were the only ones still there, and the tanks were coming down the street looking for them.

It would take sometimes an hour for her to be convinced that it was only a dream, that there'd been no siren. She'd get up and look out the windows, trying to see if there were still cars parked in front of the building. Once she had even gone downstairs and stood outside in the middle of the night in her robe to see if there was a plane flying overhead, shooting off the double red flares of warning.

She took another swallow of gin. God, it was poisonous stuff. But it did help her relax. That time she'd gone outside, looking for people, she'd come back and had a whole glassful, just so she could unwind enough to go back to sleep. And the next morning she'd had a terrible headache. That's when she discovered that a quick drink, a little one, helped with that too. Of course, she'd never normally drink in the morning, but this was an exception.

She took another swallow, looked at the level of liquor in the glass. It wasn't going to be enough, she could tell. She got the bottle out and filled the glass again to the halfway mark. Lord, Tom had looked so shocked when she'd slapped him. She felt so damned guilty about that, but she had to shut him up. She had to.

She tilted the bottle over the glass again, and watched as the last of the gin approached the rim.

"Where would you go?" Sam asked, genuinely curious. From time to time he'd gotten mad at his own brother Tom, or his father, when he was growing up. When he'd needed a place to go, it usually ended up being the barn, and sometimes he'd be so mad he'd

78

clean the milking machines just to have something to do with his hands.

Years later, he'd wondered at the timing of the fights that sent him steaming, furious, to the barn. It would be unworthy of Tom Beckett to get his little brother angry just to get out of his turn at milking-machine maintenance. Unworthy, but Tom was no fool either. Milking machines were a bitch to clean.

There weren't any milking machines in Hainerberg, as far as he knew. And Tom Robicheaux didn't look like the type who would take out his anger constructively anyway. He was slight and dark haired and fine boned, and his eyes were the same shade of violet blue as his sister's, and he was cracking his knuckles and sitting with his shoulders hunched over as if he expected a blow.

"Where would you go?" Sam asked again.

The back of Tom's head moved from side to side in negation. "I don't know. I don't care. Away from here.

"I wish she was dead instead of Aunt Jeanne."

He meant it, Sam realized. His voice was filled with simple conviction. He really did hate his mother, and really did wish her dead.

"What did she do?" . . . *this time*, he finished mentally, going cold with dread.

"She says I talked back to Colonel Elphenstane's wife, and she said I had to apologize. I couldn't go out until I did. Mrs. Elephent asked me if I liked it here and I said no! That's not talking back!"

"It doesn't sound like it," Sam agreed cautiously. "What happened then?"

"Mrs. Elephent said she thought I should like it because it was Germany. And I said I hated it because of the Russians. And Mrs. Elephent said I shouldn't think about the Russians. And I said she was dumb if she didn't because they have a bunch of tanks and they're going to come and shoot us all

79

dead. And then they're going to bomb us. It said so on the radio." Tom still hadn't lifted his head. He didn't need to for Sam to sense his bitterness and fear. He believed implicitly in what he said. So did most Americans at the time, he realized. But these Americans were, quite literally, on the front lines of a potential nuclear war, and the Americans at home would never have that experience.

He thought about the suitcases, packed in case of evacuation, and wondered how many of the American military personnel had explained to their children exactly why they had to remain within call at all times, why they had to be ready to abandon everything on two hours' notice to flee a threat that would inevitably outpace them. He wondered how many had explained to their wives, much less their children.

Probably not many. How could you explain away the news coming every day over the radio, in the *Stars and Stripes* and the *Wiesbaden Post* and all the other newspapers in all the other American duty stations in Europe? The ones who understood the full extent of the threat were bound by the classification of their knowledge. As for the rest—it was 1961, after all, and few husbands took time to explain to their wives, fewer parents took time to explain to their children. But the women and the children weren't deaf and weren't stupid, and they could measure distances on maps and look toward the horizon to see what was coming.

There were newspapers and radios. There were the orders to be ready to leave. Perhaps the officers and enlisted men assumed that that was enough, that and the orders they passed along to their families. Orders that came down the chain of command, from the President to the Joint Chiefs to the military commands in Europe to the individual units and then, inexorably, to the families.

Back in the States, they might be nervous. In Europe, and particularly in Germany, they were *there*. Their only hope was the diplomacy of the politicians and, for the religious, the mercy of God and the might of the United States military.

Trickle-down discipline, Sam thought, and squelched the phrase firmly.

"You probably shouldn't have called her Mrs. Elephent," he observed, keeping his tone as mild as possible. "If her name is Mrs. Elphenstane."

Tom raised his head at last, and a faint grin crossed his face. "She looks like an elephant. You said so yourself."

Oops, Sam thought. *Missy's no angel either.* "Well, I wouldn't say so to her face!"

The grin faded. "Mrs. Elphenstane called and told her. And Mom told me I had to say I was sorry, and I said no. So she said I can't go out because Mrs. Elphenstane is the secretary of the Officers' Wives Club and Mom would get in trouble and Daddy would get in trouble too and it would be my fault."

"Why would Daddy get in trouble?"

Tom took the opportunity to condescend to his little sister and regain his equilibrium at the same time. "She's the secretary of the Officers' Wives Club, dummy," he repeated. "She'll tell Colonel Elephent and he'll tell Dad's boss and it will end up on Daddy's efficiency report."

"What *you* said?"

Tom nodded. Pulling his knees up, he laced his fingers around them, and the cuff of the shirt slid up, revealing a yellow mark above his wrist. He caught Sam staring, and slid the sleeve up farther, staring at an old, large bruise with critical interest. "She says I have to wear these shirts until the mark goes away, even though it's hot. I think she's afraid somebody will see them and think I don't snap to fast enough."

It took Sam a few seconds to find his voice. "Isn't she afraid somebody will report her for hitting you like that?"

The look Tom gave him was honestly confused. "Report her? Who to?"

"Well . . . You could." Sam realized, uncomfortably, that he really didn't know to whom one might report child abuse in the military in 1961. He resolved to remember to ask Al about it.

"We can't report things. We're kids." Tom turned away, dismissing the suggestion with such finality that even Sam didn't want to pursue it.

"I hate her," he repeated. "I'm going to run away."

Sam was beginning to think this conversation was going nowhere. "Where would you go?" he tried again.

Tom shrugged. "Dunno. I could go to the dump, I guess. Or I could go into the park and live there."

"What would you eat? Where would you sleep?"

Tom shrugged.

"Are you going to go tonight?"

"You can't come!" Tom got up in one smooth movement and dashed the collection of plastic horses off the windowsill to the floor. "I'm going to go by myself. I'm going to do what I want to do, and not follow dumb rules and be polite all the time." He headed for the door. "I'm not going to let her hit me any more."

Grasping for straws, Sam said, "Aren't you going to wait for Daddy to come home?"

"Daddy's never coming home." Tom had one hand on the door, but he had stopped, waiting, as if he wanted to be talked out of what he'd just said.

"He's coming home tomorrow night. I heard." Six-year-olds weren't expected to be precise, Sam realized. Tom wouldn't expect Missy to be able to explain what she knew.

"Really?"

Sam nodded vigorously.

"Then I'll stay until he goes away again, and *then* I'll run away."

Not if I can help it, Sam thought. *I'm not here to stop World War Three. I'm here to stop you.*

CHAPTER
NINE

West Berlin "must be eliminated as a strong-point of the Cold War."
  —Walter Ulbricht, East German leader

Verbeena slid a large sheet of drawing paper under the Visitor's hands and placed a tin box full of loose crayons on the white table next to her. "Do you like to draw pictures, Missy?"

The tentative smile was almost like one of Sam Beckett's, but Missy made no effort to touch either paper or colors. "Yes, ma'am."

"That's wonderful!" Verbeena made herself show more enthusiasm than she actually felt. "Would you like to draw a picture now?"

"Yes, ma'am." There was a little pause. "What would you like me to draw?"

"Anything you want, honey. You choose." Her doctorate wasn't in child psychology, but she was refreshing her memory of the courses she'd taken. Art therapy was suggested for trauma. It wasn't limited to children. She was willing to try anything, at this point.

"Anything I want?" Missy said.

"Anything," Verbeena repeated.

Missy reached for the colors, keeping one eye on the doctor, and chose one. Looking down, finally, at the paper and the crayon in her hand, she hesitated. "Could I—"

The wax cylinder was red.

"Do you want another color, honey?"

Missy nodded, and her eyes—Sam's eyes—filled with tears.

"Missy, you can use any color you want. You can use all the colors, if you want. And there's lots of paper, too. You can draw as many pictures as you want. You can use it all up, and I'll bring some more tomorrow." It was difficult to keep her voice cheerful and encouraging when what she wanted to do was find the adults who had intimidated and terrified this little girl to the point that she was afraid to pick up a second crayon without permission, to the point that she was afraid to color a picture. "Would you like for me to go away while you work on it?" Find them and *strangle* them.

Missy hesitated again.

It wasn't fair to ask her to answer that question, Verbeena realized. She couldn't tell an adult to go away. "Tell you what. I'll go up the stairs to that little room." She pointed to the observation office. Missy looked where she pointed and nodded. "I'm going to do some things. When you're finished, you wave your hand, and I'll see, and then we'll play another game, all right?"

Missy nodded vigorously, and Verbeena gave her a quick, impulsive hug. The broad shoulders tensed. Verbeena planted a light kiss on the white lock of hair and let go, thinking, *Girl, I'm gonna find your parents and just purely kill them, I swear!*

She made her way up the stairs and into the observation deck, settled herself into the chair and made a show of shuffling papers. At the same time, she changed the angle of a view screen to give herself a more convenient view.

Missy was looking up at her. She waved and smiled. Missy smiled back, a little less tentative now, and reached for a crayon.

"Ziggy," Verbeena said, "show me what she's doing, please."

The screen filled with the image of a man's hand clutching a colored stick too small for it, the long fingers moving up and down, trying to find a comfortable grip. Sam Beckett had had a good eye for detail, and was a fair draftsman, but he was no great artist. His talents had always been in music.

Missy, though, had some talent. Even with the handicap of a much larger body and synapses she wasn't used to, it showed. She was drawing a house.

The camera panned closer. No, it wasn't a house after all. An apartment house, maybe: a long building with three doors, and matching sets of six windows in three pairs above each door, scaled to the proper size. Each window, except the one in the uppermost left corner, had its own window box, with dots of color to represent flowers. Missy carefully etched in a line of green for a lawn in front of the building, and then picked up a white crayon and colored in the sky. Not clouds, Verbeena noted, but a homogenous, white sky.

She stopped then, studying the composition with a tilt of the head, and then carefully put the drawing to one side.

"No people," Verbeena murmured.

"This representation is an approximation of the building in which the Robicheaux family lived during Major Robicheaux's tour in Germany," the computer responded. The image of the drawing froze and shrank to one side of the screen. The other side of the screen was filled with the image of a black-and-white photograph of a building. The resemblance was close enough to be recognizable, with the exception of the window boxes. None of the windows in the photograph had window boxes.

"I suppose this is where the family lived," Verbeena said, tapping lightly at the window in the upper left.

"That's correct, Doctor. How did *you* know?" Ziggy was sometimes displeased to be reminded that mere humans could also draw valid conclusions. It was part of the massive ego that had been programmed into it. One of Dr. Beckett's less inspired decisions, Verbeena had always thought.

"She thinks everyone else has something they don't," the doctor responded. "She thinks other people are happy. They have flowers. Her family doesn't." Glancing down at the Visitor, she saw Missy hard at work again. "What's she doing now?"

"Family," Ziggy said succinctly, still miffed. "Her skills at portraiture are consonant with her age group."

Verbeena allowed one eyebrow to rise, but said nothing. The screen changed again to show a view over the Visitor's shoulder. The picture was obscured by the hand creating it and by the other hand, which not only held the paper in place but shielded the sketch.

The drawing hand paused. Verbeena guessed that Missy was sneaking a look up at the deck, and allowed herself an elaborate yawn before looking up to smile encouragingly at the child. Missy returned the smile, and then, turning back to the sketch, abruptly wadded it up and put it on the corner of the table. She promptly started a new drawing.

"Didn't like that last one, did she?" Verbeena mused. "What's the best shot we had of it?"

It wasn't good enough. All she could see were lines and circles. Missy had kept it obscured, even from the computer's scanners.

But it was only wadded up, not torn, and instead of throwing it on the floor as any other child her age might have, she had set it aside. To be rescued later and examined by her friendly local psychologist. . . .

Missy kept it up for more than an hour before she put the scattered crayons back into the box and shyly waved a hand. Three pictures had been wadded up and set along the top of the desk. Verbeena checked the time—almost suppertime—and came back down the stairs to join the child. She couldn't let it go too long. Sam's body's need for food and sleep would be different from Missy's, but it was Missy's mind that was running Sam's body, and Missy had the mind of a growing child.

"May I see your pictures?" she asked.

The completed work was neatly stacked under Missy's elbow. Verbeena watched for any sign of reluctance as the girl pulled them forward, and saw none.

"These are very good," she said. It was not an exaggeration. Some of the pictures were clumsy, but all of them showed a level of detail, such as the flowers in the flower boxes, that Verbeena truly admired. "This one is very nice. Is this where your family lives?"

"Ahuh." Missy was a bit wary, but pleased with the praise. "We live up here."

"That's what I thought. That's a nice building." She scanned the other drawings.

There were birds and horses and trees and houses, but no people at all. "Why do you color the sky that color, Missy?"

Heavy brows knit in confusion. "That's the color it *is*."

"I always thought the sky was blue."

Missy shook her head. "No. The sky is *white*."

She was definite enough about it that Verbeena didn't want to argue. There must be some reason the child thought so. Though come to think of it, the photographs Ziggy had come up with did seem to present a uniformly drab sky. She'd have to remember to ask the computer, later on.

But it was a shame she wouldn't be able to bring Missy up to the surface of the Project, take her out to run around the buildings and look up into the brilliant, pure blue. Missy would have to stay in the Waiting Room, just in case Sam accomplished whatever it was that he was supposed to do, so he could Leap again.

And if Missy and the world survived, maybe someday she would be able to see the blue New Mexico sky with her own eyes anyway.

"I suppose you didn't like these," Verbeena said. She reached out and scooped up the rejected drawings and put them in the pocket of her lab coat before Missy could protest. "I'll take care of them for you."

Later, over a dinner of her own in the tiny cafeteria the Project boasted in the cinderblock building on the surface, she smoothed the first drawing out and positioned it so that Al could see it too.

"Yeah, so?" he said, sipping at a cup of coffee and making the ritual grimace. "Stick figures."

"These are the only pictures of people she did."

Al poked at the sheets, separating them. "I don't know anything about art, but I know this isn't very good."

"She's only six, Al. Not even that, really. Her birthday's this month."

Al shrugged and looked again. The first picture showed four figures, two small, one, set farther off, medium sized, and the fourth much larger, looming over the two small ones.

"Mommy and Daddy and the kids," he said. "So?"

"So, very small kids, very very large Mommy who's holding on to them by the shoulder. And there's Daddy, with his hat over his eyes, far away. And look at this second one. Nobody's smiling. And the third one . . . Al, none of them even have a face. But in every one, Mommy's holding on."

"I'm not a child psychologist, but I think there are some obvious conclusions we could draw here."

90

"Are the obvious conclusions always the right ones?" The oven in the cooking partition cheeped, and Al got up to retrieve a pair of pot pies. Returning, he put one in front of Verbeena, one in front of himself, and muttered, "I know the *real* reason Sam Leaped out of here. He was looking for a decent meal."

Verbeena chuckled and cracked the pastry shell, allowing steam to escape. "I offered to cook, you know."

"Verbeena, if one of us is going to cook, I'll do it, okay?" He stabbed his own pot pie. "With all due respect, your cooking is even worse than this stuff."

Verbeena shrugged.

"The point is that there's information here that we may be able to use to help Sam."

"And maybe help Missy, too, eh?"

"Well, of course." Al stuck a forkful of steaming mush into his mouth and yelped, none too discreetly.

Verbeena ignored his frantic efforts to cool his burned tongue. "Ziggy said there was a ninety-four percent chance that Sam was supposed to prevent World War Three."

Al nodded vigorously, finally getting the food down. "Yow. I mean, yes. Ninety-four percent."

"So there's a six-percent chance he's supposed to do something else."

Al looked disgusted. "You don't shoot craps, do you, Verbeena?"

"No, why?"

"Or play poker? Or blackjack?"

Verbeena gave him a fond, exasperated look. "You're saying the odds are against it."

"I wouldn't bet my retirement pay on six chances out of a hundred."

"But didn't you say that Sam doesn't think that's why he's there, either?"

91

"Oh, *Sam*." Al waved his hand dismissively. "He gets all kinds of ideas about why he's Leaped someplace."

"And he's usually right, isn't he?"

Al stopped in mid-wave and looked at her. "Whose side are you on, anyway?"

"Missy's. Sam's. Yours, really."

"Have you looked outside lately?"

Verbeena shuddered. "No, thanks."

The Project existed in the moment of time in which it *could* exist: a slice which, at the moment, was exceedingly narrow. Those really drastic changes in the timestream which threatened the very existence of the Project slipped it "sideways" until things settled down again. So far, things had always settled down. No one wanted to think about the consequences if they didn't. Meanwhile, the continuum of "sideways," outside the perimeters of the Project, was—chaos.

Someday they would consider the whole subject in detail. But not. Right. Now.

"But that's my argument, you know," Verbeena went on. "Either Sam saves us, or it doesn't happen to begin with, because if it had, we wouldn't be here."

"It must have been Sam's feminine side that programmed Ziggy," Al snarled to himself. "Nobody can twist logic like a woman." He sighed and rocked his head back, staring at the ceiling. "Okay. Ziggy, humor the lady."

"It's a legitimate question, Admiral," Ziggy snapped. "There's no need to be patronizing."

Al rocked forward to look at Verbeena. "Am I patronizing you, Verbeena?"

Verbeena smiled with real humor, well used to his particular quirks. "You wouldn't dare."

Al nodded emphatically. "Damn right. Ziggy? If the end of the world doesn't happen, what *does* go on?"

92

"Besides us," Verbeena added.

There was a pause, while the computer extrapolated the history of the world from an unknown. It took some time, even for Ziggy.

"There is a steadily increasing chance that Missy Robicheaux will be placed in a foster home within the next two weeks."

"What?" Verbeena and Al chorused. "How does that fit in with your end-of-the-world scenario?" Verbeena continued.

"What happened to her father? Did he get shot at the Wall or something?" Al's focus was slightly different.

Ziggy heaved a very human, very artificial sigh. "As you know, Admiral and Doctor, we deal with more than one set of possibilities at a time. This is a new aspect of a second-order set of possibilities, of which I felt you should be aware. To answer your question, Admiral, Major Robicheaux retires from the military in a Reduction in Force in 1967."

Al's brows knit. "He didn't get promoted?"

"The impact on the major's efficiency report was such that he was not considered promotable. The major is still alive today, however, having retired from a second career with a national accounting firm."

"And what happened to Mrs. Robicheaux and Tom?" Verbeena asked.

"And what had an impact on his efficiency report?" Al said.

"It seems that Tom Robicheaux ran away from home. That may or may not be related to the event recorded on the efficiency report, which you must admit would impact the major's efficiency: Mrs. Robicheaux's suicide."

Al and Verbeena stared at each other.

"He gets that tendency to melodrama from Sam, too," Al said sourly.

CHAPTER
TEN

" . . . the U.S. and its allies must hold on to West Berlin even if it means a nuclear war with Russia. . . . Western civilization is in greater danger now than at any time in the past."
—Sam Rayburn, Speaker of the U.S. House of Representatives

"*How* does she commit suicide?" Sam asked as he clattered down the steps into the apartment building basement. It was deserted on this late Sunday afternoon. Sam, finally away from the apartment and on his own, had decided to explore.

"Pills and alcohol, Ziggy says. Nobody knows whether it was deliberate, a reaction to the death of her twin, a response to the pressure of being here, or just another stupid accident. But the kids go to a foster home because their father has to be away so much and there's nobody to take care of them, and when he retires, he makes a deal with the foster parents to keep them." Al was watching the handlink with fascination as the possibility of the end of the world receded with every step down that Sam took.

"Which probability set is this?" Sam inquired,

peering down the dark stairway and fumbling for a light switch.

"Second order."

Sam nodded, as if dismissing the news. Al knew better. He had a habit of appearing to ignore the obvious in order to chase down the details first. It was only an appearance.

"Hey, what else is down here?" Sam said at the foot of the stairs.

Al looked from the handlink to the area around them. "Over there are the storage cages," he said, indicating the chain-link gates that went from floor to ceiling. There were six of them, one for each apartment in the stairwell. One stood empty, the door gaping; the rest were stuffed to various degrees with boxes, trunks, suitcases, and the odd piece of furniture collected by families who moved at least every three years and didn't always have the time, inclination or financial resources to get rid of everything and start over fresh every time.

"Over there—"

"Laundry room." Sam hopped down from the last step and stuck his head around the corner. The smells of wet laundry and soap were like a slap in the face.

It was a large, gray concrete room, badly lit by the evening sun shining through paper-lined clerestory windows. Lines of wet laundry dripped from wall to wall, creating panels of white sheets and towels and underwear. Along the wall, three washing machines stood empty, waiting for new loads.

"The maids' quarters are down this way." Al floated past the storage cages.

"The laundry room is as big as the storage area *and* the maids' quarters?"

"Put together," Al affirmed. "Hey, don't blame me. I didn't approve the blueprints. Besides, it doesn't look like anybody's home anyway."

Al floated through the walls to look. It was true.

96

The maids' quarters were the same size as the storage cages, perhaps big enough to hold a military folding cot and a weathered dresser and a stove. A very small stove. But no maids.

"I don't suppose you can tell which one is Marta's," Sam said, running to the end of the little hallway and back again.

Al raised an eyebrow. Sam had a disconcerting tendency sometimes to take on characteristics of the people he Leaped into. Running up and down might not be something the adult Sam Beckett would normally do, but a six-year-old with too much energy would.

And the adult Sam Beckett would never, never peek through a keyhole in an effort to see into someone else's bedroom. That was behavior Al reserved for himself. "Wait, this is it."

"How do you know?"

"Pictures on the dresser. Looks like Marta with a little girl about your age."

Sam grimaced and straightened up again, remembering adult dignity. "Do you know where Marta is now?"

Al poked at the handlink. "Nope. No records. But this is interesting . . . Ziggy's found some stuff in the old East German Staasi files. Seems our Marta is an agent, all right, but she isn't really a pro. She's got relatives in the old country."

"Are you serious?"

"Absolutely. But you gotta remember, Sam, in this case the old country is less than three hundred miles"—he looked around to get his bearings, pointed through the laundry room—"that way.

"Marta's one of those people who got co-opted by the various Soviet intelligence services to collect information on American military personnel. She's not doing it because she's a committed Communist; she's doing it because she has parents in East Germany, and her daughter is there with them. And she picks up some extra money, too."

"So she takes military information?"

"Sam, she's got no commitment to us. And she doesn't have any idea what the stuff is, anyway. They give her a camera, she takes pictures, they give her money. If she gets enough money, maybe she can live in a place that's a little bigger than a shoe closet someday. Marta's a good capitalist at heart."

"There's something sick about a system that makes people spy on other people," Sam muttered, kicking the wall.

Al, remembering the level of security required at Project Quantum Leap, said nothing. If Sam didn't remember his own security clearance, well . . . maybe he'd remember the next time.

"When is she going to get back?"

Al consulted the handlink again. "Well, Ziggy doesn't exactly have her schedule down—otherwise we wouldn't be down here in the first place—but we could try again in an hour or so."

"What happens in an hour?"

Al shrugged. "I don't know. I don't think Ziggy does either. Things are a little vague."

The handlink squealed. Al snorted. "Smartass computer," he muttered. "Actually, maybe it has something to do with getting transportation back into the area. Ziggy thinks that Marta may be off visiting friends, or maybe even her controls. But she needs to be back here in about an hour, or she won't be able to get back at all."

"So the others will be coming back soon too," Sam speculated.

"Hey, that's right. Maybe they all went out on the town. Hey, where are you going?"

"Out to play."

Al watched as the small girl/adult man marched back up the steps and out the door.

Hainerberg was a relatively new housing development. None of the trees were very old, though they would look taller from the perspective of a child. A long slope, good for winter sledding but for now still covered in green, led down to the next building. A line of low bushes with dark green leaves and bright red berries lined the top of the slope.

Sam followed the sidewalk down the length of the building. The stairwell with the Robicheaux apartment was Number 21; the building also contained stairwells 19 and 17. The only thing that distinguished it from every other building in sight were the numbers by the front door.

Past the end of the building were more bushes and a fenced playground containing a swingset, a slide, and a large concrete-edged sandbox. Tom was sitting on the side of the sandbox, deep in discussion with another boy his own age. Sam wandered over to the swings, the better to keep an unobtrusive eye on him. He got into a who-can-swing-higher contest with another little girl, who gave it up after a while and went away in a huff, without speaking to him.

"What do the second-order probabilities indicate on the kids' future?" He sat on the wooden board seat, beginning to swing idly back and forth, scraping his feet on the ground. "Since we *have* to assume they have one."

The Observer tapped a button. "Hmmmm. Missy still ends up as a psychologist. Never gets married. Tom . . ." Al slapped the handlink. "It keeps going in and out. Now it looks like Tom's a mechanic, has a wife and two kids."

Sam shook his head. "So if I'm here to save the world from blowing up, and Tom from running away, and their mother from committing suicide, it's so she can go on abusing them?"

Tom and the blond kid had their heads together over something of great interest inside the sandbox. A blue shimmer in the air between them caught Sam's eye. The two boys were playing with fire, holding lighted twigs up against the sky, waving them around. The flames went out on one small branch, and the blond boy pulled out a box of wooden matches and lit it again.

"Or perhaps to hold the family together. I don't know, Sam. This is a tough one."

Shadows were beginning to stretch across the playground. A few other children came in, looked around, spotted Tom and his friend, and hastily went elsewhere.

"He isn't very popular, is he?"

"Nope. I think he's basically a good kid, Sam, it's just that . . . oh-oh."

The boy with Tom was nudging him and nodding toward Sam. Tom was resisting some suggestion.

"So maybe if Tom doesn't run away, his mother won't attempt suicide—" Sam continued, oblivious.

"We don't know that it *was* suicide, Sam. And I think you'd better pay some attention to those little devils." Al was punching in a query to Ziggy as he spoke.

"What devils—"

But by this time the two boys were swaggering over to the swings.

"Hey, Missy," Tom's friend said.

Something about his tone of voice got Sam's attention. He was a pale blond boy with nearly invisible eyebrows. Tom was hanging back, letting the other boy take the lead.

"What do you want?" Something about the kid made Sam's skin crawl. If he pushed away from the two boys, the movement of the swing would take him closer. He didn't much want to be closer. Either one of the boys was bigger than Missy; the two of them loomed over him.

He wasn't much used to being intimidated by someone else's size. He wasn't, in his own body, particularly bulky, but he was quick and fit and well trained in several martial arts. He'd never lacked courage.

But he wasn't in his own body. Missy wasn't fragile, but she was a child, and she'd learned to read the body language of the people around her, particularly when it came to potential threats. That body language meant trouble, and that was why Missy shrank away. The conflict between his host's gut knowledge and Sam's mental abilities got him into some interesting situations.

This was one of them.

"We want to see your panties," the blond boy sneered.

"Oh, no," Al groaned. "This is Walt Davis, Sam. He's bad news."

Sam flicked an *Oh, really? What a surprise!* glance at Al, then turned his attention back to the boys.

Sam looked at Tom. Tom looked away.

The blond boy poked at Sam, reaching for the waistband of Missy's shorts. Tom refused to look his sister in the eyes.

"Don't touch me," Sam said sharply.

"Whatcha gonna do, scaredycat?" Walt punched Sam/Missy in the arm, hard. "Come on!"

"You little proto-rapist," Al snarled. It was a good thing the Observer was a hologram, Sam thought fleetingly, or he would have drop-kicked Walt right out of the playground.

Sam twisted out of the swing. Missy didn't have the reach he was used to, but on the other hand, Sam didn't have the mental limits Missy did. When he hit, he expected to be able to use the power of an adult male. Missy wasn't an adult male, but that belief certainly exercised everything her frail body was capable of, both in terms of the impact to his opponent's stomach and in terms of running away.

Al hung around behind to see what happened. Walt doubled up and collapsed. Tom stared gape-jawed after the image of his fleeing kid sister, and down at his friend, and decided to pursue neither Missy nor the issue. He leaned over to talk to his friend. Al nodded smugly. "Gushie, center me on Sam."

But there were still limits to what a child could do, no matter what its mental abilities. Sam was hanging on to the front door to the stairwell of number 21, chest heaving like a bellows, face alarmingly red. It took a long five minutes before he could reach up and push one of the buttons beside the nameplates.

Somewhere inside the building, a doorbell buzzed. There was no answer. Sam tried again, swallowing spittle.

Again, there was no answer.

Sam took another moment, making sure that his breathing was normal before he tried to talk. "Al, go up and check, will you?"

Al looked over his shoulder, back down the line of the building toward the playground. There was no one in sight.

He hit the button. Ziggy and Gushie, monitoring, centered him on Mrs. Robicheaux.

Mrs. Robicheaux was passed out on the floor in the master bedroom.

Al stared down at the body sprawled in front of him. One hand was twisted in the fringes of the bedspread, dragging it loose from the pillows. Her mouth gaped open, and she snored, loudly.

Lips pressed into a thin line, Al shook his head. "It wouldn't do any good to shout at you even if you could hear me," he muttered. "How could you let this happen to yourself? How could you let it happen to your husband and kids?"

The body on the floor didn't answer.

Al punched in a realignment on the handlink, and appeared next to Sam. "It isn't going to work," he said, "she's in no condition to press the door release . . . Sam?"

Sam wasn't paying attention. Abruptly, Al realized why. Walt and Tom were coming up the walk.

The blond kid was still walking carefully, but the look in his eye was unmistakable. Tom, beside him, was talking to him, his words rapid, urgent, and completely ignored.

"This looks like more trouble."

"No kidding," Sam muttered. He had his breath back, but the original blow plus the panicked run had taken a lot out of the six-year-old body. Besides, there was no place else to go.

He started hitting other buttons beside other names, any other names.

"That's going to get her into trouble," Al observed.

Sam gave him an incredulous look and pounded on the buttons again.

A staticky voice came through on the speaker. "Who is that? Who's down there?"

"It's Missy, and I really need to get inside!" Sam yelled.

The boys heard. Walt grinned and started moving faster. Tom put out one hand to stop him, or at least slow him down, and was shaken off without a backward glance.

"You'd better quit ringing my bell, or your parents are going to hear about it!" The speaker clicked off.

Sam punched the bell again. "Please!"

"I'm going to report you if you do that one more time!" This time the speaker didn't bother to ask who was ringing.

By this time the boys were standing in front of the doorstep. Walt had an ugly grin on his face, not improved by the fact that he'd recently lost a baby tooth in front. Tom was looking at the windows of the apartments with an expression comprised equally of uneasiness and anxiety.

"What's the matter, Missy, don't you have any place to run?"

"If you don't leave me alone, *you're* gonna get reported," Sam said, turning to face his tormentor. "I didn't do anything to you."

103

"Yeah, well, we're gonna do something to you, aren't we, Tom?"

Tom bit his lips. "Walt, people can see," he said. "Come on, leave her alone."

"She hit me!"

Sam at least had the satisfaction of hearing Walt admit he'd been hit. Al was still muttering over the handlink and glaring uselessly at the two boys. "You deserved it, you little bastard," he muttered.

Walt stepped forward, crowding Sam back into the doorway, out of the line of sight of the apartment windows. He kept his eyes on Missy's hands, clearly not willing to risk another slug to the stomach.

Sam feinted to his right, twisted, and hit the door buzzers again.

The doors remained closed.

Far away, a recording of a bugle sounded, playing "Retreat." A car on the street pulled over. Even Tom and Walt seemed to hold their breath for the duration of the melody. "Retreat" ended, the National Anthem began, and Walt snickered.

"There's somebody getting out of the car," Sam said desperately. "Leave me alone or I'll scream."

Walt looked over his shoulder. It was long enough for Sam to shove desperately at his shoulder, trying to knock him off balance and clear a path to run. But Tom was standing in the way, offering no real threat but acting as an obstacle nonetheless, and this time Walt had been prepared. He hit back, and Sam went flying against the closed door.

"You little jerk!" Al exploded. "Who taught you you could hit a girl!" He spun on Tom. "Why aren't you sticking up for your sister!"

One part of Sam's mind wondered about the equity of that particular rule, while the rest of it wondered whether the person getting out of the car was going to notice what was going on, and stop it. The people in Hainerberg seemed to have developed the art of keeping out of other people's business to a very high level indeed. He wished somebody would descend to his level for a minute or two, or at least long enough to keep him from being beaten up and stripped half-naked by a little ten-year-old savage with a yen for little girls' panties. *He'd* never been like this when he was ten.

"Hey! Walt!" Sam could hear the urgency in Tom's voice, warning his friend off. "Walt, quit it."

At the same time he could hear Al, standing practically inside the door behind him, saying, "It's Marta. She's back from wherever she went. She'll stop it."

"She's only a maid," Walt snarled, as if in answer, and reached for Sam again.

CHAPTER
ELEVEN

"You are going to arm the Germans with nuclear weapons. You talk about reunification, and the German people do not want to reunify . . ."
        —Soviet Ambassador Mikhail Menshikov

Sam saw Walt's blue eyes widen in shock as Marta's heavy hand descended on his shoulder and clenched into the fabric of his shirt. "What you boys doing?" she asked, her accent even more pronounced than usual.

"Go away," Walt said, reaching for Sam again.

"*Nyet!*" Marta said, pushing the boy away. His eyes widened, and he kicked at the woman. She grunted and moved herself in between Sam and the two boys. Walt cursed and ran away, yelling, "You'll be sorry!" as he went.

"Sam, that did it!" Al was staring at the datalink, practically sputtering with excitement. Sam opened his mouth to ask what did what, but Marta had him by the shoulder, was pulling out an old-fashioned key ring, unlocking the door, and herding him inside.

Tom was following, hesitantly. Marta turned on him. "What do you think you will do?"

"Not—nothing. I'm not going to do anything. I'm sorry if Missy got scared, I tried to tell him to stop it. People were watching!"

"You think this is good reason? That people watch?" Marta wasn't impressed.

Tom shut up, confused. It *was* a good reason, Sam realized, from Tom's point of view, and the point of view of Tom's parents and Tom's peers. It might not be the only reason, but Tom wouldn't understand Marta's rejection of it. Marta motioned Sam up the stairs, trudging after, her heavy steps echoing in the stairwell as they made their way up the paired flights of stairs. Tom trailed along behind, dragging one hand along the stairwell railing and looking miserable.

Marta had a key to Apartment 5 as well. She searched through the keys on the ring, holding them up to the light, and finally picked the right one. Al, choosing not to wait, floated through the door before it was opened.

Sam entered the apartment, stepping around the suitcases, with considerable relief. He wondered how often Missy had had to fend off Tom's friends.

But not, at least, Tom himself. Missy's brother cleared his throat and said, "Look, I'm sorry, Walt shouldn't have done that. It won't happen again."

Sam, who had apologized to a little sister once or twice himself, appreciated the effort. "That's okay. He's gonna be mad, though."

"He sure is, Sam," Al chimed in. "He's going to report Marta as a spy."

"How?" Sam asked Al.

Marta snorted again, her opinion obvious.

"Walt always gets mad when he doesn't get his way." Tom, who thought the question was directed at him, also felt he was explaining the obvious. "Where's Mom?"

Marta glanced at the closed master bedroom door and said nothing.

"She's in there, Sam. Passed out on the floor. You don't want to go in there, and neither does Tom."

"I think she's taking a nap," Sam said hastily. He cast a worried glance at Al; but Al, who had seen quite a few drunks in his time, waved a hand at him reassuringly.

"Don't worry about her, Sam. She's going to wake up with a hell of a headache, but that's it."

"Sure she is." Tom didn't believe "Missy's" convenient story, but made no effort to check.

He must be used to having his mother "take a nap" at odd moments, Sam thought. He shook his head and went over to the radio in the living room, making a mental note to look in on the woman later on, when there would be no one to witness a girlchild trying to remember how to act like a medical doctor. He was inclined to accept Al's expertise in the matter, but he'd still feel better if he checked Mrs. Robicheaux's vital signs himself.

Tom disappeared down the hall, into his own room. Marta surveyed the dining room area critically and went into the kitchen. The sound of running water announced that she wasn't satisfied with the way someone had done the dishes.

"What do you mean about Walt reporting Marta?" Sam said quietly over his shoulder to Al as he fiddled with the ivory radio dials. He found a station playing classical music, and the sounds of Beethoven came softly from under his fingertips.

"He tells his father what she said, and his father reports it." Al was scanning the handlink. "Walt's father—uh-oh. He reports it as carelessness on the major's part, allowing his wife to hire a Russian. Marta gets fired immediately, of course, and held for questioning. She never gets to steal the papers. The probability set that contained the war just evaporated. It never happens."

"So why haven't I Leaped? There *is* something else I'm supposed to do, isn't there?"

Al chewed vigorously on his cigar. "Well, it looks that way. When that little bugger—I mean, Walt—tells on Marta, there's the alert—the major loses his place on the promotion list. And it all starts with the suicide. Maybe that's—"

"Wait a minute! What alert? What did Marta say?"

"Oh. Yeah. I forgot you didn't know this yet. There's an evacuation drill tomorrow night. That's when Mrs. Robicheaux takes too many pills and booze, and dies. Great timing, huh?"

Sam closed his eyes and leaned his forehead against the smooth brown plastic of the radio case. "That's it," he says. "That's what I'm supposed to do. I have to save her."

Al nodded reluctantly. "You said yourself that if you do, the abuse will continue."

"It's the stress, Al. I don't think she's deliberately doing this. But look at what's going on in this woman's life: She's just had a death and can't even get home for the funeral, her husband is gone, she doesn't know exactly where or why, except that it has something to do with this crisis; she hears all about the international tension, Khrushchev's speeches and the replies from the Americans and French and British, and she knows that Russian tanks are on maneuvers less than one hundred miles away. All those sabres are rattling right next to her, she's in a foreign country with two young children, and the world's about to blow up, and there's nothing she can do."

"And people are watching," Al quoted dryly. "Appearances are everything for the good military wife. I guess the surprising thing is that more of them didn't crack."

"You can't blame her," Sam went on. "She's trying to do the best she can. Her kids aren't helping much."

"They're kids, after all. Kids think that whatever their circumstances are, is normal. They don't have the experience to know any different."

Sam shot him a glance. Al had said things, from time to time, about his own youthful "circumstances." Sam wondered if the Observer really grew up thinking he was in a normal environment. An orphanage, pool halls, theatre. . . .

Of course, being Al, he would have fled anything resembling a normal life anyway. Al was the type to fill life's cup brim full, slurp it down, and look for a chaser.

There was one little point that still escaped him. "What did Marta say?" he asked. "What's Walt going to report, anyway? It's not like it was the first time he'd ever seen her. He knew who she was. What makes this time different?"

"Oh, that. She said 'nyet.' "

" 'No'?"

"In *Russian*, Sam."

"She'd get fired for saying one word in Russian?"

"Remember what you were just saying about those tanks?" Al pointed out. "One word is all it takes. It wasn't so long ago that Joe McCarthy had people in cold sweats for sitting next to the wrong person in church. Somebody actually speaking Russian was presumed to be a spy. And remember, she actually *is*."

"But that's not her fault," Sam argued. "And besides, she protected me from Walt."

"Nothing is ever anybody's fault," Al snapped. "But somehow, things still happen, don't they? What are we supposed to do, let her get away?"

"I think so."

Al fell silent, recognizing the look on Sam's face. He could be amazingly stubborn when it came to Doing What Was Right. Probably, the Observer thought, sulking, that was the reason he was picked by Whatever was the motivating force behind the

Leaps to begin with. If there was ever a person who was appropriate for setting things right that once went wrong, Sam Beckett was that person.

"Do you think if you warn Marta, you're going to Leap?" he asked.

"No. I never have felt this end-of-the-world stuff had anything to do with this Leap. It's just something I should do." With that, he squared his host's shoulders and marched into the kitchen. Al followed him, shaking his head.

Marta was elbow-deep in dishwater. One sink was full of suds; the other contained water that once was clear and now was dotted with islands of bubbles. The kitchen smelled of hot water and vinegar.

"Marta?"

Marta glanced at him, took a plate out of the soapy water and swished it back and forth in the rinse water, examined it critically, and set it in the drainer. She was wearing thick yellow kitchen gloves that sent a pang of nostalgia through Sam for a moment; his mother used to wear gloves like that when she did the dishes, too.

"Yes, what is it?"

It took a moment for Sam to realize that the maid wasn't speaking English any more, but German. It added considerably to her fluency. He answered her in the same language, startling her into immobility.

"Marta, I know what you're supposed to do here, and I think you should know that Walt—that boy with the yellow hair—is going to tell his father that he heard you speaking Russian."

"I speak no Russian," Marta spat, turning to face him and peeling off her gloves. She towered over Missy's slight figure. "I hate the Russians. I'm a good German."

"But they've got your parents and your little girl, don't they? And even if they didn't, it doesn't matter. When you were warning Walt away, you said 'nyet.'"

112

"One word, only. You Americans think having several languages means I am a spy, because you only have one." Her heavy brows beetled over small, dark eyes. "But you're speaking good German. How did you learn so quickly?"

"That doesn't matter." Sam was hedging, and Marta could tell. "What matters is that you were supposed to take some papers from Major Robicheaux, weren't you, and give them to someone. But Walt's going to tell his father, and they're going to come and take you away for questioning."

A look of utter blankness, a solid wall, descended over the maid's heavy features. She stood very still, staring at Sam without expression, for a very long moment.

"How do you know this?" she said at last.

"It doesn't matter how I know, does it? It's true."

"I will not let them take me away," Marta whispered. "But my little girl—they have my little girl—" It wasn't clear, in her words, just who was going to be taking her away and who had her child. So far as Sam could tell, it didn't matter. Police could operate under different flags and serve different economic systems, but they were still, always and forever, Police. They were always the knock on the door in the dead of night, and Marta clearly feared both sides equally.

Sam and Al exchanged glances. "Sometimes you just can't win," Al said quietly, even though there was no chance that Marta could hear him. "If Marta is arrested, who knows what they'll do to her family. If she isn't, but just quits, well, we don't know that either. There aren't any records. The Staasi were pretty thorough in some places about getting rid of evidence when the Wall fell."

"Marta," Sam said gently, "I just thought you should know what Walt's going to do. I can't tell you anything about your little girl or your parents."

Marta stood in the middle of the kitchen floor, water dripping from the gloves in her hands. "Do you speak Russian, too?" she asked, suddenly, harshly, in that language.

Sam hesitated, nodded. "Yes, I speak Russian," he answered in kind.

Marta asked a question again, presumably about another language in that language. It was one that Sam didn't know, so he remained silent.

Marta smiled grimly. "So even demons have their limits."

"Maybe the police do too."

"You are not Missy. Missy has no German, no Russian. Who are you?"

"That doesn't matter, does it?" Sam took a deep breath, not wanting to get into a discussion of the Project at this point. "If you take the papers from the Major, there will be more trouble than just getting arrested. *I'll* tell him what I heard you say."

"My mother is Russian," Marta said. "But she's not a bad person. It's not her fault. She had a hard time here, after the war. Germans don't like Russians. It was easier for her and my father to stay in the eastern zone."

"No, of course she's not bad. I understand, Marta, really. I'm not condemning you. I'm just letting you know."

"They wanted to stay," she went on. "I thought I could get more work if I came here. I do good work."

She was explaining herself, Sam realized. Offering justifications, not to him, but to the police she expected to come for her. Rehearsing what she would have to say, even though she believed it would make no difference.

"They let me go," Marta went on in a whisper. "But they kept my little girl. They said I could work for Americans and earn a lot of money, and my parents and my Frisel would have a home and good

114

food. There is no food in the east."

Sam kept silent. Marta looked at him a while longer, then pulled her gloves back on and turned back to the kitchen sink, draining the cold wash water and adding hot, finishing the dishes. "I am supposed to give notice," she said over her shoulder. "Fifteen days."

"There isn't time," Sam told her.

She nodded without turning around. "I give my notice to you, then. Yes?"

"Yes."

The handlink chirped as Al asked for data.

"Ziggy says that she finishes the dishes, goes down to her room, packs, and disappears. Nobody ever hears from her again."

Sam asked a silent question. Al picked up on it. "We don't have any data about her family, Sam. I'm sorry. They just drop out of history, as far as Ziggy can tell. The spooks check into Walt's report, but she's gone before she could do any damage, so they don't follow up on it either."

It was unexpectedly painful not to know. He was used to finding out what happened to people, to having the flash of satisfaction in knowing that at least there was some redemption, if not actually a happy ending, before he Leaped. But this time there was no information and no Leap, either. He would never know if telling her had been the right thing to do. There would never be any feedback on this one from anything except his own conscience.

In the long run, that was enough. It had to be.

He turned and left the woman behind.

There was Mrs. Robicheaux to check on, still. He eased open the door to the master bedroom and looked around, catching a glimpse of "himself" in the mirror above the vanity. Despite himself, he tried on a smile to see how it looked on Missy's features. It looked like any other smile assumed for the occasion, minus a right incisor. He shrugged and knelt by the recumbent figure of Missy's mother.

She had curled up by this time and was asleep, snoring softly, her head pillowed on her left arm. Sam felt under the curve of her jaw for her pulse. It was dull and steady. He took a pillow off the bed and slipped it under her head, wondering meanwhile what would have happened if he had tried to pick her up and someone—Tom, for instance— had come in. He wished sometimes that it had been his body that Leaped, not just his mind, or soul, or awareness, or whatever it was. It would certainly be convenient in terms of situations like this one.

On the other hand, it would have been hell finding Bermuda shorts to fit.

Maybe in some other timeline it had happened that way, and somehow the clothing problem was solved, but he was in *this* timeline and had to cope with its limitations.

He shrugged again and straightened Mrs. Robicheaux's legs and dress, took the bedspread off the bed and spread it over her, tucking her in. It didn't seem likely she was going to move for the rest of the night. There was no sense in letting her get a chill.

"Sad, isn't it?" Al said, as Sam brushed his hands free of lint.

"I'm not sure sad is exactly the right word." Sam looked around, decided there was nothing more he could do to make the woman comfortable. "Okay. Now, where do we stand? What does Ziggy say history looks like now?"

Al peered at the handlink. "Now Ziggy thinks that the Major comes in tomorrow afternoon, stays a few hours, and leaves again. There's an evacuation drill tomorrow evening, but the Robicheaux family doesn't make it to the Eagle Club—that's the assembly point. The day after tomorrow, in the morning, Mrs. R is found dead in this apartment of a combination of pills and alcohol. A fairly understandable scenario,"

Al added, cocking an eyebrow at Mrs. Robicheaux. She muttered softly to herself and snuggled deeper into the bedspread. "Missy's here. Tom's gone. Oh—"

"Oh what? What happened to Tom?"

"They find Tom's body in a utility shed, dead of smoke inhalation." Al touched a series of the colored cubes in careful order. "Now Ziggy says you're here to save Tom. Probably . . . This is weird, Sam. Ziggy can't decide whether Tom lives and grows up to be an engineer, or dies in that fire. It looks like it's up to you. Ninety-four-percent chance."

Sam, who had heard those particular odds quoted before, gave him a look of pure exasperation. "Is there *anything* stable about this Leap? What about his mother?"

Al shook his head. "As close as we can tell, the deaths happened just about the same time, Sam. So you could save one or the other of them, but not both. I'm not sure how you're supposed to do that, though."

"Was there something specific that triggered the incident? Why did she take the pills?"

Al shrugged. "Who knows? Stress? An evacuation drill might have set her off."

"Was that when they would have grabbed the suitcases?"

Al nodded. "They'd set up pontoon bridges across the Rhine and the other rivers, and the military personnel would report for duty. Their wives had two hours to corral the kids and throw everything they were allowed to take into cars and get to the rendezvous points."

"Over *pontoon bridges*?" Sam asked incredulously, trying to imagine his mother, Thelma Beckett, driving the Robicheaux station wagon across a pontoon bridge.

"They were in a hurry, Sam, and the existing bridges couldn't carry the traffic."

"What if they couldn't find the kids? If they were out playing, or at a movie, or—"

Al took a deep breath. His gaze met Sam's unflinchingly, mercilessly. "They left them behind."

CHAPTER

TWELVE

"Our partners and friends are making all preparations to resist. . . ."
—Konrad Adenauer, Chancellor of the Federal Republic of Germany

"Those are the facts," Al said. "I don't like them any better than you do. You don't like them any better than any military man. We're talking about *their kids,* you know. But you can't hold up a military operation because a kid gets lost. Even if it's your own."

" 'War is not healthy for children and other living things,' " Sam quoted softly.

"So to speak," Al said. There was a certain barrier between himself and Sam on this subject. Al was career military. Sam preferred a nonviolent solution to problems wherever possible. Al might consider that his first option, but he was prepared to back it up with a destroyer fleet and a couple of aircraft carriers if necessary.

"So did Missy get lost too?"

Al queried Ziggy. "No. She got picked up by the military police and turned over to the block wardens."

Sam looked down at Mrs. Robicheaux, who was smiling now in her sleep. "It doesn't seem right that she'd be dead thirty-six hours from now. Or Tom either."

"Nope." Al chewed ferociously at his unlit cigar. "On the other hand, if she dies, at least the kids won't be abused any more." At Sam's glare, he added hastily, "I mean, if one or the other of them is going to die, if you can only save one, that's something you have to think about."

"I don't think they'd be abused if she was out of here. She's so worried about the political situation and how what she does will affect her husband's career, it's no wonder she's on the thin edge."

"Well, she fell over it, and all the king's horses and all the king's men couldn't put her together again."

"You sound like you've already written her off. Isn't that a little cold-blooded, even for you?"

Al looked hurt. "Sam, there's only one of you. You can't be in two places at once, even with me helping. If you've got to make a choice—"

"I don't think I do." Sam rarely got angry, but when he did it went deep and stayed hot. Usually, the things that got him angry were things that got to Al too—blatant injustice, cruelty to the helpless, senseless waste. Every once in a while, though, the two hit something on which they disagreed on the most basic level. In such cases, oddly enough, it was usually the normally peaceful Sam who got angry at Al, rather than the other way around. Al might get excited and wave his arms and yell, but he rarely, very rarely, truly lost his temper at Sam.

He wasn't about to do so now, mostly because he could recognize and understand Sam's frustration. "Look, Sam, you can try, but if you can't save them both, you have to think about which one gets the effort. It's exactly like medical triage. You use all the resources available to save the ones that can

120

be saved. Otherwise you're going to lose them both, and what good will that do anybody? Missy ends up in foster care. Besides, the chances are good you're going to save Tom. In at least one future he grows up to be an engineer, remember?"

The sound of the front door opening and closing again came from the front of the apartment. Marta was leaving. Al hiked his eyebrows, looked at Ziggy again, and nodded to himself.

"Look, whatever you do, you can't do any of it tonight," Al said at last. "You may as well go to bed. Tomorrow looks like it's going to be a hell of a day."

Unwillingly, Sam agreed.

"I just wish things would settle down," Al complained later to Verbeena. "You'd think we could pick up a telephone book and check to see if the guy was listed, and that would be our answer." They were back in the dining room, which had taken on its evening character as a gathering place for Project personnel. At the moment, that meant that two technicians were comparing dress materials in a corner, and another was noodling at the keys of a battered piano on the other side of the room.

Verbeena was the only person Al had ever told about the shifts in history—the different pasts that he and Ziggy could remember. Verbeena was always a part of their present, and the past she recalled was always the most recent one as if it had always been, but she was a good listener. And unlike Ziggy, she was human and could understand the gut frustration and unspoken fears that worked on the Observer.

It was almost as if the moment Sam took his first Leap, the entire Project had, in an equal and opposite reaction, been plunged into temporal flux. The longer Al spent with Sam, the more likely it was that something would be different when he left the Imaging Chamber and came back into the Project itself. Usually, the changes were very small, sometimes hardly noticeable. The professional aspects—Verbeena being the Project psychologist, Gushie being chief programmer, Al as administrative director and Observer—never seemed to change, perhaps because they were so necessary to Ziggy's functioning. But the personal relationships were subject to flux. This time, Tina and Gushie were married. Since Tina was the current love of Al's life, this made things difficult.

Al couldn't even tell Tina about how things changed. How could he explain to her that sometimes she was his lover, and sometimes she was Gushie's wife, and sometimes she was carrying on with Gushie behind Al's back, and every time he came out of the Imaging Chamber he had to check with Ziggy to find out who the players were and who they were playing with this time?

Verbeena, for her part, suspected that one of the fears that Al lived with was that someday he'd come out of the Imaging Chamber and find that Verbeena herself had changed. She recognized, intellectually, that that might have already happened, several times, depending on what Sam did to change things at any particular time. But that way lay madness, and Verbeena's job was to fend it off, not to explore it for herself. Fortunately, she had a well-grounded sense of who she was. No matter *what* Sam Beckett did.

By definition, the only thing that would remain stable in any particular Leap would be the identity of the individual in the Waiting Room. Verbeena was taking advantage of Missy Robicheaux's six-year-old energy by making sure that Sam Beckett's body danced and jumped rope and ate a perfectly balanced diet. It was better than keeping the body sedated all the time. She was able to feed the child's voracious curiosity with games, puzzles, simple physics experiments, and the ever-popular

122

crayons, meanwhile distracting her from the fact of the body she was in.

It was a good thing that Missy *was* only six. Her span of attention wasn't that long to begin with, and Verbeena and her assistants were able, with a long-practiced matter-of-factness, to let her know that there was nothing particularly strange or horrifying about her being in a man's body. Because she was a child, she took her cues about what was awful from the adults around her. Verbeena was hoping that would mean no trauma for her later. She just hoped the child retained the self-esteem they were trying to instill. Verbeena went around these days with her fingers more or less permanently crossed.

"So Sam's sleeping safe?"

"Bet you can't say that three times fast." Al tried to smile. It was a decent effort, all things considered.

Verbeena gave him a get-serious glance, and he capitulated. "Yeah, he's asleep. Tomorrow Missy's dad comes home for a flying visit, and about three hours after he leaves, all hell breaks loose. He needs all the sleep he can get." He nodded in the general direction—down—of the Waiting Room. "How's . . . um, Missy doing?"

Verbeena smiled. "Have you ever watched little kids running around and wished you had that kind of energy?"

"Yeah, so?"

"Let's put it this way: Sam's body is getting a *lot* of exercise." She chuckled. "I still wish I could bring in my nieces to play with her. She's a sweet kid."

"Are you still worried about psychological damage?"

The chuckle was wiped away, and Verbeena chewed on her lower lip. "So long as the people around her don't make an issue out of it; so long as we treat her like a child, without particularly emphasizing *girl* child; so long as it doesn't last too long . . .

123

I don't think there's going to be lasting damage."

"Why don't you want to emphasize that she's a girl?"

"Because first and foremost, she's a *child*. But at the same time, she's not stupid. She believes she's having a long dream where she's a grown-up man, even though she knows that's not really possible. We don't want to keep reminding her of the impossibility of the situation." The doctor drew a long breath. "In the long run, it might even be beneficial for her. As she's 'pretending' to be a man, we're encouraging her to explore options. One of the problems female children have had, historically, is the idea that because they're female, there are certain things they can't do in their lives. The early sixties were very repressive. I hope that she remembers playing with a stethoscope as a doctor instead of assuming that she'd have to be a nurse."

Her face closed off for a moment, and Al, watching her, realized that Verbeena Beeks herself had been about that age in the early sixties. She had faced externally imposed restrictions not only because she was female, but because she was black as well. She would have grown up during a time when African-American cultural awareness was brought to the awareness of the whole country. Al wondered how many people had tried to tell Verbeena Beeks that she'd have to settle for something other than what she really wanted.

"Will she remember?" Visitors tended not to recall their stays in the Waiting Room; the same swiss-cheese effect that scrambled Sam's memory made hash out of theirs, too. Which helped explain how they didn't know what Sam had been doing in their bodies when their backs were . . . well, not turned, exactly, but . . . Al gave up. Metaphors were not his long suit.

"Probably not," Verbeena conceded. Across the room, someone was trying out some honky-tonk on

124

the piano, without much success. "But we're hoping to plant a seed. Who knows?"

"Who knows?" Al agreed. Whoever or Whatever had Sam Leaping, presumably. Al hoped that *Somebody* had a plan.

"Oh, there's Tina. Will you excuse me for a moment, Al? I need to talk to her before she and Gushie go to Phoenix." Verbeena got up and crossed the room to speak to a tall, leggy redhead who was standing next to a somewhat overweight man with a thin mustache. Al watched the ensuing conversation, hoping that his feelings weren't showing.

It had been a shock to click out of connection with Sam, returning to the relatively drab Imaging Chamber, only to have Ziggy inform him that Tina and Gushie had gotten married last month, and he himself had given away the bride.

It was as if there were a million timelines out there, a million of Sam's strings, and on every one of them marched an Al Calavicci. And every time he came back to the Imaging Chamber, he came back on a slightly different timeline, and had to integrate a new version of his memory. He loved Tina, he was almost sure. It really hurt to see her with somebody else.

He consoled himself with the thought that the timelines seemed to re-cross themselves with regularity. Next time he looked in on Sam and then came back, it was likely that Tina would be single again, and ready to pick up where they left off time before last. It would be a lot easier to deal with, though, if his "absences" were more than just walking from one room to another.

He didn't actually "go" anywhere when he looked in on Sam; that was the maddening part. He just walked up the ramp, through the airlock and into the Imaging Chamber, and called on Ziggy to trigger the link created by the shared neural network on Ziggy's biochips. In less than the blink of an eye, he was "there," wherever Sam was, sharing his perceptions of his surroundings, his consciousness catapulted back to whatever time Sam's was Leaped to. Ziggy had created the "Door" to the Imaging Chamber as a concession to both Sam and Al, so that they'd have a cognitive marker for the transition between the Accelerator part of the Project's Imaging Chamber and wherever Sam was, but it wasn't real.

Nothing was real when time wouldn't stay put.

But it would be very nice if he could figure out how to nail down certain elements of it, he thought longingly as he watched Tina swaying her way out the door.

However, nothing could be done about it right now. He looked at his watch and rubbed his temples. It wasn't all that late, but he wasn't sure what he could do next. Go talk to Ziggy? The idea lacked appeal. Go back to his own office and do paperwork? The idea *definitely* lacked appeal. They were nearing the end of the fiscal year, and reports had to be prepared and next year's budget worked on, capital equipment funds *had* to be spent by the first of the month, there were rumors the G.A.O. was interested again.

Sam had Leaped away from more than bad cooking, blast him.

But that was what he was paid for. That and keeping track of Sam in time. Sighing, he got up and headed for the exit, leaving behind him the sound of honky-tonk and technical chatter.

Monday, August 7, 1961

HEADQUARTERS
7100TH SUPPORT WING
WIESBADEN AREA COMMAND
INFORMATION AND INSTRUCTIONS
FOR NONCOMBATANTS
IN THE EVENT OF AN EMERGENCY

4. **ACTION UPON ALERT:** (cont'd)

d. Noncombatants will utilize civilian vehicles for transportation and move under the control of Wardens and/or Deputy Wardens to predesignated supply points and then to areas of safety. Individual private vehicles will not be permitted to travel alone but must be incorporated in convoys proceeding under military control.

f. Noncombatants will be limited to one light handbag and two (2) blankets per individual. No persons will be evacuated (maids, etc.) who are not authorized noncombatants.

CHAPTER
THIRTEEN

"A statement issued by the United States, France, Britain, and West Germany warned Russia not to overrun West Berlin. . . ."

Sam Beckett woke up on Monday morning, August 7, to the sound of an Armed Forces Radio announcer comparing Gus Grissom's space flight the month before and Titov's current journey. He listened, wondering, as the announcer portentously concluded that space travel would never last because of the deleterious effects of weightlessness lasting more than seventy-two hours.

The next topic was the increase in the flow of East German refugees. "Analysts believe that the end of the German school year has enabled German families to leave their homes under the guise of taking a 'vacation trip.' East German authorities refuse to acknowledge that their people are fleeing the repressive political system of Communist rule. Meanwhile, more than seventeen hundred refugees were registered in the Marienfeld Camp in Berlin this weekend. Many refugees indicate fear that the Communists are about to close the Berlin escape hatch. Others have decided to leave because of party pressure to speed up work in factories and on farms. Central party authorities are pressing all the way down the line for more work to overcome shortages—including the labor shortage helped by the flight of refugees."

The radio crackled, shut off. The bedroom door swung open without a warning knock. "Missy, get up. I don't know where Marta could be, but you've got to eat breakfast. I've got a Gray Ladies meeting in less than an hour. Come on, please."

She sounded sober and rational. She looked sober and rational and very tired, with dark circles under her eyes inexpertly covered with makeup. She was wearing a baggy gray dress that looked almost like a uniform, with red crosses on the blunt collar points. She stood waiting, one hand on the doorknob. "Come *on*, Missy. The eggs are getting cold."

One of the sacrifices Sam had to make, Leaping into other peoples' lives, was pretending to enjoy things he normally hated. Soft-boiled eggs, for example. Finally dressed, he came into the dining room to find a white egg cup decorated with yellow roses waiting for him, with a spoon and napkin beside it. Steam rose from a bowl of eggs.

"Sit down and eat," she said. "Lord, I'm never going to get out of here on time—What are you looking at?"

"Nothing," Sam muttered, sliding into his seat. He used the spoon to ladle an egg into the egg cup, made a face, and cracked it. "Small end or big end?" he said under his breath as he rotated the cup, tapping carefully. People declared war over the strangest things. Eggs. Walls. "Something there is that doesn't love. . . ."

"What did you say?" Missy's mother had finished eating already, was setting a plate with two slices of toast, carefully buttered and cut diagonally, down on the table in front of her daughter. "Did you say something?"

"No. Nothing." Sam wasn't inclined to explain the connection between breakfast and satire. It was too early in the morning to pretend to be six. Too many impossible things before breakfast—but no, that was Lewis Carroll. He kept on tapping, thinking that he really wasn't being too swift this morning.

"Sometimes I think you're just crazy," she said. "Talking to yourself like that. What will people think of you?"

Something in her tone made Sam look up quickly. She was staring at him, her fingers were curled around the top rung of the chair next to him, and for one frozen moment he felt like a deer, spotlighted out of season.

"I think you're just crazy," she repeated.

He didn't know what to say. The edge of the spoon touched the egg, tentative: Tap? Once again, when the woman said nothing—a little stronger, as if operating by itself, not as anything under his control: Tap? Tap?

"Damn it! Stop playing with your food!" Jane Robicheaux's hand swept down and caught at the egg cup, twisting it out of his hand and sweeping it in a wild arc at the far wall, splattering yolk and albumen and shell and china in a wide pattern. Sam had no time to duck away. The woman snatched for the collar of the blouse he wore, dragging him up the back of his chair until he was choking against the top button, and her other hand slapped at him, back, forth, one side of his face and then the other, repeatedly, as she kept on screaming, *"Damn you! I told you I was going to be late, but you don't care! You don't care about me! You little monster, monster, monster, how dare you sit there and make fun of me! Stop it!"*

He was clawing at the top of the blouse, trying to loosen it, trying to let himself breathe, trying to deflect the blows raining down on him, and the words were becoming a blur. He kicked, frantically,

131

and his foot managed to get over the top of the table. It only gave her more leverage, and she pulled harder, and his other leg came up until they were both thrashing, kicking, knocking the bowl of eggs to the floor, kicking the glass off the table, and she continued to scream at him, continued to hit him, with her fist this time.

"You little bitch, you selfish inconsiderate little bitch, look at what you've done, look at it, look at it, damn you, damn you, you're going to clean that up, you're going to clean every bit of that up, you little monster!"

Quite suddenly, it was over. His ears ached with the sudden silence. His eyes were closed to protect them against blows no longer falling. The hand twisted in the back of his collar lowered him to the table—his struggles had brought his entire body up—and the fingers loosened, slowly, as if circulation was slow to return to them.

He kept his eyes closed. He could not imagine what might happen next.

What happened next was the sensation of the blouse being tugged down into place, the wrinkles smoothed away as if to erase what had just occurred, and Jane Robicheaux's voice again, quiet, a bit raw, saying, "You see what you make me do when you play with your food like that? Look at all this mess. You're going to clean up this mess for Mommy, aren't you?"

He dared to look, dared to peek from between rapidly swelling eyelids, to see her looking down at him with an expression of patience, of understanding, of tolerance, of sympathy leavened with firmness, and he thought, *She's fucking insane!*

"I wish I knew where Marta was," Jane fretted, straightening. "She ought to be up here by now to do the dishes and the beds. I don't want her helping you, though. This mess is your responsibility, understand?

"If that Tom doesn't get up soon, he's going to have to go without his breakfast, and he's going to be cranky all day." She moved away to the sideboard and picked up a pair of gloves and a hat. "I'm going to call him. Now I don't want you two fighting, do you hear? Last time I thought Captain Jessup was going to report us, the way you two carry on. So you be nice, you hear?"

Sam thought the warning might have been better directed to Tom, but held his peace, rolling off the table and falling to the floor, picking himself up again as fast as he could, almost slipping in the ruin of eggs from the bowl.

"Now, don't expect me to fix you another one, not after the way you've wasted all this food. Look at this mess." She shook her head.

Sam stared at her, wide-eyed and incredulous. The way *he* had wasted—? But she seemed to see nothing the least bit incongruous either in her words, or in the change in her manner from raging Fury to exasperated, but perfectly calm, mother.

Sam started to shake his head in negation and stopped. It hurt. Possible concussion, he thought. "No, thank you. One is enough."

"Well." Jane slapped her hands against her dress. "You do remember your manners after all. That's wonderful. Why couldn't you do that last week at the Jessups'?"

Sam ducked his head, unable to make any response about what Missy might have done last week. Apparently her mother didn't require or expect an answer.

"I'm going to put the key up here. If you go out, you'll have to take it with you, or if Tom takes it you'll have to stay with him if you want to get back in. Do you understand?"

"Yes, ma'am." Somehow, based on yesterday's events—had it only been yesterday?—Sam didn't think that depending on Tom for safe access to the

133

apartment was a good plan. He kept a wary eye on the woman as she rummaged in her purse for the keys. It would take all day to clean up the mess, anyway, he thought, and he didn't want to go outside anyway and expose the new collection of bruises he could feel cropping up to the curious gaze of the neighbors. He thought she had knocked a tooth out, too.

On the other hand, he needed to figure out a way to keep Tom from running away.

On the third hand, perhaps running away was an excellent idea, and he ought to be helping Tom with his escape plans.

The woman looked around, dissatisfied, as if sure she had forgotten something important. "I should be home by lunchtime. Tell Marta to fix sandwiches. I need to get to the commissary on Saturday." Her voice trailed off. Then, as if a new source of energy had opened up, she marched over and gave him a kiss on the cheek. "All right. I've got to go to my meeting. You be a good girl, all right? I'm going to ask Father about a novena for—" her breath caught in a sob, and she took a deep brave breath and began again—"about a novena for Jeanne. Put the dishes in the kitchen for Marta, get this mess cleaned up, and I'll be back in a little while, okay?"

"Okay, Mom," Sam whispered.

He no longer felt guilty about addressing strangers by intimate names. It would be far more distressing, and far more awkward, to explain why he didn't. He had to play the role he was dealt as well as possible.

Even this role.

He wasn't sure what Missy would say to her mother next, though, so he kept quiet. The door closed behind Mrs. Robicheaux, and he breathed a sigh of thanks. Now all he had to do was clean up and deal with Tom. After yesterday's experience—after this morning's—he'd rather do that without adult witnesses.

The door to Tom's room was an inch or so ajar. He knocked, gently enough to keep from opening it farther.

"What?"

"Can I come in?"

There was a short, amazed silence. Sam couldn't imagine *his* little sister asking for permission to come into his room when he was growing up, either. She either came in, or wouldn't be caught dead there.

The door opened, and Tom stood in the doorway. "What do you want?"

Sam couldn't quite see past him. "I want to talk to you about what you said yesterday."

"What do you mean, what I said? I said I was sorry already." He looked at his sister appraisingly. "She got you pretty good, huh?"

Sam shrugged and waited. He was still shaking. He did *not* want to talk about it.

Tom stepped back at last, and Sam followed him in.

The first thing that struck him were the model planes hanging from the ceiling, fighters and bombers and transports. The bedspread was covered with pictures of airplanes. The rug in the middle of the room had an outline of an airplane. A half-completed model occupied the top of the dresser. The room smelled of glue and patience.

A well-stuffed knapsack hung on one of the bedposts.

"You said you were going to run away," Sam said, eyeing the knapsack.

"Yeah, so? You can't come."

Sam closed his eyes. At the moment, the refusal sounded like one more door swinging shut, trapping him even more firmly in the body of a battered child.

"I don't want to," he said at last, though it took more courage than he knew he possessed. "I want to tell you not to go."

Tom looked at him with a mixture of utter disdain and disbelief. "You can't tell me what to do. I outrank you. I'm older than you are."

Sam wished passionately he'd found someone else to Leap into. "If you run away, what will Mom do?" he said, trying to put the argument in terms that Tom would understand. "She'll get really mad then." *She'll beat her daughter to death.*

Tom understood. He paused, and said, "She won't hurt you. She'll be mad at me. Only I won't be here."

Sam refrained from pointing out what would, to an adult, be obvious: that when the target of anger wasn't present, the target of convenience would do. The part of his mind struggling to remember that *he*, Sam Beckett, was an adult speculated that Jane's outburst was due to her anger and pain from the news of the loss of her sister. It didn't help.

"What happens if we have to leave and you're not here?" he appealed next.

Tom shrugged. "Don't care."

"You'll get Dad in trouble."

Tom shook his head. "I just want to get out of here. I hate her."

"She's your mother. You don't really hate her, do you?"

"Yes I do!" Tom met his eyes. "You do, too."

"No I don't!" Sam denied. And it was true, he realized; he didn't hate Jane Robicheaux. He feared her, but more than anything else he pitied her.

Tom went over to the dresser, opened a drawer, and pulled out a pair of socks. He stuffed them into the knapsack. "What are you looking at?"

"Where will you go?"

"I'm not going to tell you."

"Is Walt going too?"

"None of your business."

"Walt's talking you into this, isn't he?" Sam said, a light dawning. "You're doing this because he says so."

"Am not. Get out of my room." Tom was shifting mental gears, becoming defensive and territorial, and he was going to turn on his little sister any moment now. Sam backed down.

"Well, you could at least wait until after Daddy gets home," he said, and immediately regretted the words. Al had *told* him the boy ran away after his father left. What had he done, ensured that the event he was supposed to prevent would in fact actually happen?

Tom paused. "You said that before. What makes you think Daddy's going to come home? He's in Berlin or someplace."

"He's coming home tonight." Maybe he could say something to the Major, let him know there was impending trouble. "I heard Mom say so." He was improvising. He spent most of a Leap improvising. Usually it worked better than this.

"Oh, Mom. You don't believe *her*."

"Why not?" It didn't seem reasonable that Missy wouldn't believe what her mother told her. It didn't seem reasonable that Tom wouldn't, either. She might be abusive, but she was first of all Mother, and they were her children. Sam wondered if Jane realized that she had already battered her son's trust to death, even if he himself was still alive.

"They wouldn't tell Mom if Daddy was coming home," Tom explained. "They don't tell families." But he had stopped packing long enough to look at the model on the dresser. Unlike most of the other models, which were of contemporary aircraft, this one was of an antique biplane. Sam came over to look at it more closely, reached out without thinking to touch a wooden strut. Tom hit his arm away, with impersonal force.

"That's mine. Keep your hands off."

"I wasn't going to break it," Sam protested. "I just wanted to see."

"It's mine," Tom repeated. "Leave it alone. I keep telling you not to touch my stuff."

"Okay, okay." Sam put his hands behind his back, signaling concession. "I was just looking."

Tom looked as though he expected more of an argument. When he didn't get it, he turned back to the model and touched it lightly. "It's almost done," he said.

"You can't take it with you if you run away."

Tom's hand dropped away. "I don't want to go," he admitted, talking almost to himself.

"Then don't."

"But I hate her! I hate being yelled at!"

And, Sam thought, he hated watching his mother drink, and he hated being hit and watching his little sister be hit. Tom hated being watched, as they had been watched in church the day before, being mentally graded and assessed and used to grade and assess their parents. He hated the pressure of so many eyes. He wanted to run away from the eyes.

Sam could see it, could understand it, and couldn't begin to explain to him that running away wouldn't get rid of the staring eyes; if anything, it would make things worse.

Always assuming, of course, that he even survived the experience of running away, which according to Ziggy wasn't going to happen. Death by fire. He shuddered, sick at the thought.

Once, Sam had been caught in a house fire. He had Leaped out before the roof collapsed on him. Sometimes, still, his swiss-cheese memory tossed the memory up at him, the heat and the terror, the smell of burning and the choking sensation of smoke filling up his throat, and the image of burning timbers descending upon him. At odd moments he wondered about the altruism of Whatever made him Leap, of Whoever had gotten him out of there only to replace Sam Beckett with the original owner of the body. Clayton Fuller had taken a fiery death

138

for him. He hoped that the Leap had cut things closely enough that Clayton didn't have time to feel the terror he had taken with him on his Leap out.

He didn't want to think that Tom would find himself in the same situation. Sam was pretty sure that Clayton had died when the burning roof beam collapsed on him. If Tom died of smoke inhalation, it meant that he would probably be alive and conscious long enough to realize he was trapped with no way out. Sam desperately did not want that to happen. He didn't have the first idea about how to prevent it. He wished Al would show up.

"Daddy's coming home tonight. Why don't we tell him then about how Mom hits us?" he repeated.

But the very words seemed traitorous, and he wondered how any child could bring himself to "tell" on a parent. Especially one like Jane Robicheaux. Again, with the split vision he so often experienced recently in Leaps, he could sympathize, with an adult's understanding, with the pressures on the woman without condoning her actions. As a child, looking through a child's eyes, he could only see the results.

"I don't believe you," Tom said flatly, and returned to randomly pulling clothing out of the dresser and stuffing it into the knapsack. "I don't think he's coming at all." When the sack overflowed, he pulled everything out again and scattered it on the floor. "Tell Marta not to come in here," he said, getting on his knees and sorting through the debris for a toy airplane. It was the first thing to go back into the bag.

"Marta's not coming back. She's gone."

That stopped Tom again. "What do you mean, she's gone? She's right downstairs. Boy, you're dumb."

"She left. She had to go—Walt was going to tell on her. He was gonna tell his father she was a spy." He paused, thought about this. "Which she was," he added, to be scrupulously fair.

"You're making things up. Mom's gonna wale you again, you keep making things up like that."

"Am not." Sam had no idea how to explain how he knew what he knew. Being able to retreat to a child's responses made life a great deal easier. Nobody expected a child to explain.

Except another child. Tom continued to pack.

"Mom went to her Gray Ladies meeting, so you don't have to run away right now, do you? You could wait 'til later and see if Dad comes home." At this point Sam was willing to take this Leap one minute at a time. "You could eat breakfast first."

Finally, he'd hit on a suggestion that got through. Tom dropped the knapsack. "Come on, then."

He wasn't going to let Sam remain in his room. This was fine with Sam; obediently, he followed Tom out to the dining room.

The room was still a mess, with rapidly drying egg on the walls and floor. Tom shook his head. "We better get this cleaned up, huh?"

Sam glanced at him gratefully. Tom had to have heard Jane's shouting. The two of them buckled down, wetting down dish towels and wiping up the mess as best they could. When they finished, Tom looked around and announced, "I want cinnamon toast."

"Oh, good," Sam exclaimed. "I love cinnamon toast."

What the hell. It would keep Tom off the streets.

CHAPTER

FOURTEEN

" . . . the West fears Khrushchev is orchestrating a showdown over Berlin . . ."

Mrs. Robicheaux came home for lunch, as promised. As she came in the door, the test sirens went off, rising and falling. She and Sam both stood transfixed, listening, counting off the seconds. When the siren died down, at the end of one minute, both of them heaved sighs of relief.

Tom was out playing. At least he'd left the knapsack behind, so Sam felt fairly secure that he was planning on coming back.

"Where's Marta?" Jane said, stripping off her gloves.

Sam didn't feel up to explaining things. He occupied himself with setting forks carefully to the left of the plates, hoping that this evidence of preparedness for lunch would soften whatever explosion might come.

"Didn't she even come in today? Good Lord, can't I depend on anybody for anything?" She was standing in the doorway to the kitchen, having barely given a glance to the stains where the eggs had been.

Sam glanced around and winced. He and Tom had done their best to clean up the eggs; but then there was the toast. He'd tried to clean up after the toast blitz too, truly he had. But there were crumbs on the floor, and Tom had put the butter too far up on the counter for him to reach to put away, and there was a certain crunchy feel to the kitchen floor from the unswept sugar.

"This place is a pigsty! If we had an inspection right now I would die, I would just die! Look at this bread!"

They'd forgotten to put away the bread, too. Sam found himself shrinking back against the wall.

"It's going to get moldy! I'm going to have to throw it away! Do you think money grows on trees? We can't afford to buy a new loaf of bread every time you think you want a piece!"

She sounded angry, but not irrational. Sam found himself watching her every move. Her black patent leather purse dangled from her right hand, casting back reflections of the table, of the plates, of Sam backing hastily away, out of the dining room.

But she wasn't screaming. Hyperventilating, yes; her breath was coming faster and faster. Her free hand fumbled for a chair, pulled it out from the table, and she collapsed into it, looking around at the dining room and kitchen as if she had never seen them before and they were horrifying and all her responsibility. "I was going to have the Gray Ladies over for tea this afternoon," she said. "I was going to invite them into *this house*, this mess."

At least "this mess" wasn't nearly as bad as the mess she'd left behind this morning. But it didn't look like Jane even remembered the morning's incident. Sam didn't think the way the place looked now was *that* bad. The counter needed to be cleaned up, and the floors could stand to be swept, and the garbage needed to be thrown out—the eggs were getting a bit ripe in the August heat—but there was nothing ten minutes of brisk activity wouldn't take care of. "They're not coming?" he asked.

"No." Jane swallowed incipient rage. "No, they aren't coming. They decided they needed to be at home." She heaved a deep, shuddering sigh. "Thank God for small favors. All I'd need is to have Mrs. Morrison show up with those damned white gloves of hers. She thinks she can pull an inspection any time she likes, damn her." She looked over at Sam, apparently not even seeing her daughter's puffy cheeks, split lip, half-closed eyes. "You mustn't repeat that, Missy. Do you understand?"

"Yes, ma'am." Sam stepped around the voltage transformer and edged to the other end of the table. "Do you want to have lunch, Mom?"

"I suppose." She didn't look enthusiastic. "Where's Tom?"

"He went off to play."

"He knows he's supposed to check in, doesn't he?"

"Yes, ma'am." Tom hadn't said anything about "checking in," but Sam wasn't going to say so now. Jane Robicheaux looked almost normal again. She set the purse on the table, opening it and rummaging for lipstick.

"Well, do you want a sandwich?" she said, almost cheerfully.

"Yes, please."

"You have such lovely manners sometimes, Missy. I just wish you could be this way all the time."

No you don't, Sam thought. *Believe me, you don't.* But he said nothing, and stood by patiently as the woman went into the kitchen, took out more of the much-maligned bread, and made peanut-butter-and-jelly sandwiches, diagonally sliced, with the crusts carefully trimmed.

Missy got half a sandwich with a glass of milk. Her mother got the other half, plus a whole sandwich, and a glass full of clear liquid that smelled of juniper berries. She refilled the glass, and never finished the first half-sandwich.

Afterward, she went back to the master bedroom, muttering something about changing out of her Gray Ladies uniform. She staggered a little as she walked, but the wall was there to catch her. Sam got up to take the plates and glasses back to the kitchen, putting the untouched food on a separate plate by itself. Tom might actually check in, and if he did, he could have it. It wouldn't go to waste.

And there was a broom in the pantry. He got it out and began to sweep, awkwardly. There was no dishwasher, but at least he could get the sugar up off the floor. The broom was longer than Missy was tall, and awkward to maneuver, but with concentrated effort he managed to produce a small pile of dust and sugar and cinnamon. A brush would be nice, but he couldn't find one. He pushed the debris into the dustpan with the broom and a sense of triumph.

He was beginning to wonder where Al was. It would be nice to know a little more exactly when the Major was scheduled to show up, and for how long, and if the Observer had any good ideas about how Sam was supposed to convince Tom to stay home and his mother not to drink, they'd be most welcome.

Come to think of it, Sam would take any ideas at all, good ones or not. He wasn't even sure Tom would come back to check in, knapsack or no knapsack. The whole idea of checking in probably was related to the possibility of an alert, but Tom wouldn't see it that way.

He wondered if they'd ever gone through an alert, and if so, if the exercise was successful. He wished Al were around to ask.

He hated having nothing to do.

One red block on the yellow block. One blue block on the red block.

The hand that belonged to Sam Beckett fell away from the blocks. Missy Robicheaux sat cross-legged in front of the little tower and stuck out a lower lip.

"What's the matter, Missy? Is something wrong?" Verbeena got up from the rocking chair she'd had installed in the Waiting Room, set aside her crocheting, and came over to squat beside her. Sam's body bulked large beside her, but she patted Missy on the back as if the child were still in the body she was born in.

"I'm too big to play with blocks," Missy said. "Blocks are for babies."

"I know," Verbeena said, sympathetically. "We don't have very many things here for a little girl. What would you like to play with instead?"

Missy turned Sam's head and looked Verbeena in the eyes. "Am I really a little girl?" she said.

A chill trickled down Verbeena's spine.

"Of course you are, honey."

"I don't feel like a little girl."

Oh, Lord, help me with this one, Verbeena thought. "No, I don't suppose you do." She sat down beside Missy, crossing her legs to mirror the other's position. "Can I tell you a story, Missy?"

Missy looked at her, the need to say *No!* clear in her expression. But she was obedient, and she nodded. Verbeena reached out and smoothed back a stray lock of hair from the broad forehead.

"Well. Once upon a time, there was a very smart man whose name was Sam. . . ."

Later, she met Al, Tina, and Gushie in the Project's main conference room. The room was sterile, white, and would hold fifty; the four of them clustered at one end, near the coffee machine, as if seeking warmth. The fifth member of the meeting liked the cold, and was invisible anyway, at least in this room.

"You told her everything?" Tina said, her brows knitted as if completely befuddled by the concept. "Is that, like, safe?"

Verbeena sighed. "I don't see what else I could have done. Do any of you have any better suggestions?" She looked challengingly from one to the next. Tina still looked confused; Gushie clasped his hands together and smiled nervously, chewing on stray mustache hairs; and Al said nothing, stirring his coffee with a plastic mixer from a Las Vegas hotel. It was something to do with his hands, since he had put neither milk nor sugar into the drink. He wouldn't meet her eyes. If it were anyone else, Verbeena would suspect that he felt guilty of something, but in Al . . . he probably did feel guilty of something, but what the hell.

"She probably won't remember, when she Leaps back," he said. "I don't think any harm has been done. I mean, she didn't get hysterical or anything when you told her, did she?"

"No." Verbeena got a cup for herself and sat down in one of the swivel chairs, rocking back and forth in half-circles as she studied the rest of the Project's top management. Tina, who helped design and build the computer; Gushie, who programmed it; Al, who was one of its two fathers: members of what Verbeena somewhat irreverently thought of as the Project's Board of Directors. All exceedingly bright people, almost as bright as Sam Beckett himself. And like Sam Beckett, not one of them had any idea what to do about the human problems their creation had engendered. "I told her what happened, and told her she was having an adventure, but it would be over soon and she'd be back in her own body."

"What did she say?" Gushie wanted to know. He was wringing his hands now. Verbeena wondered sometimes what Tina saw in him. She was much more Al's type of woman, and Al wouldn't even look at her. Al could be very old-fashioned sometimes, Verbeena thought. He didn't mess around with married women.

146

"She wanted to know when. I told her nobody knew."

"Then what?" Al said, setting aside the well-stirred coffee without drinking it.

"Then she wanted a mirror."

There was a collective indrawn breath. "Did you give it to her?" Al had a knack for getting to the point.

"Yes, I did."

"What did she *do*?" Tina was horrified and fascinated.

"She looked."

Missy had looked. She had reached out with Sam Beckett's hand to touch the little makeup mirror the tech kept in the observation deck desk—quite against regulations—to touch the reflection not her own. Verbeena had stopped breathing as Missy froze in mid-motion, incredulous, and then completed the gesture, watching fascinated as hand met image of hand in the mirror. It was not her hand, but it moved like her hand. Neither image nor flesh looked like her own, but she could feel the cool smooth surface of the glass.

Then, focusing on the face in the mirror, Missy had wrinkled Sam's nose, waggled his eyebrows, opened his mouth wide, grimaced and made faces, touched the image in the mirror and the face reflected there, and she had laughed. "It's like Halloween," she said. "It's like a Halloween mask."

"Yes it is," Verbeena had agreed with overwhelming relief, and thinking that while Sam wouldn't be overly flattered by the comparison, he'd certainly understand it. "Just exactly like a Halloween costume. It's just one you can't take off yet, okay? But you will, real soon."

"She didn't seem too upset," Verbeena continued, returning to the present. "She was willing to accept the explanation I gave her. I'm going to continue to monitor her, of course. I'd really like to have the best available data from Ziggy."

"If you change therapy, it may change her choices when she returns to her body, and her history will change accordingly," the voice from the ceiling interjected. "The data available on Missy Robicheaux is correspondingly—fuzzy." Ziggy, the invisible fifth member of the meeting, sounded dissatisfied.

"Data on all our Visitors is fuzzy while they're Visiting," Gushie added, trying to be helpful. "Because their future is in flux until Dr. Beckett accomplishes whatever it is he's supposed to change, our past is in flux too."

"Do we have any better ideas on how to get him home?" Al asked. "Maybe then our past will stop fluxing."

"Al, is Sam under some kind of particular stress in this Leap? More than usual, I mean?" Verbeena said, looking at him curiously. "You seem to be upset."

Al shook his head. He was dressed relatively conservatively today, in a deep purple suit with black pinstripes and a black shirt. The only vivid color was a fine silk tie, heavy, expensive, beautiful, fluorescent purple with tiny bright pink squares and circles. The tie was one of his favorites.

"No. I just wish we could make more progress on getting him back. I'm tired, and if *I'm* tired, I know he is too. He never gets a break." He pulled a long cigar out of an inner coat pocket, rolled it back and forth between his fingers. "I wish we knew what keeps him from just Leaping back. It's like some kind of wall he can't get over. It's nuts."

"There's something he has to do," Tina said, with an assurance none of the rest of them felt. "When he does that, then he can come home."

"But why all this stuff in the meantime?"

"Well, maybe he has to fix all the stuff around the stuff he has to fix," she said, after a small pause to work it out. "It's like one of Gushie's programs. You have to get all the subroutines right first."

"Then why can't the subroutines be a little more routine, dammit!" Al snapped.

They all fell silent, looking away from each other.

"Are we satisfied about what Sam has to do in this Leap?" Verbeena asked.

"There is a ninety—" Ziggy began. Verbeena raised her hand, and the computer shut up.

"Al?"

Al shrugged, stripping the cellophane wrapping off the Muy Grande. "First-order probability now is that he has to prevent Jane Robicheaux's suicide, and Tom's death by fire. But I'm not sure we know what that actually *changes*. I mean, they live, but other than that, it doesn't seem that they actually make a huge difference. It's a dysfunctional family." He shrugged, baffled. "I mean, it sounds cold, but there it is."

"How big a difference makes a difference?" Gushie asked. From a programmer, it was a logical question. Al opened his mouth to answer it, and then closed it again.

"It would make a pretty big difference to me if I were alive instead of dead," Tina pointed out. "Even if I never did anything important with my life." She smiled radiantly at her husband. Al winced.

"Okay, okay. It makes a difference," he conceded. "Now will somebody tell me how Sam's supposed to *do* it?"

CHAPTER
FIFTEEN

" ... East Germans are fleeing the country at the rate of one a minute. ..."

It was a problem that Sam had been working on, too, in spare moments. He hadn't realized how full a small child's day could be. After cleaning up the kitchen, he went looking for liquor bottles, planning to pour out all the alcohol on the theory that Jane couldn't get drunk if there wasn't anything for her to drink. There was quite a lot of it: six new bottles of gin, one of Scotch and three large bottles of wine. He had them all lined up on the kitchen counter beside the sink, and was struggling to open one of the gin bottles, when he heard a key in the front door.

He recognized the man in the blue uniform from the picture in the bedroom. Steve Robicheaux was tall, thin, athletic, and gave the impression of being at attention even when leaning over to set down his battered leather briefcase beside the family's suitcases. Sam hesitated, feeling uncomfortable about yelling "Daddy!" and running into the arms of a complete stranger. Instead he stood back, hands behind his back, and waited for the man to look up and notice his daughter, waiting.

Apparently, reticence was appropriate. The major straightened up, caught sight of her, and a fleeting glint of shock lit his icy blue eyes for a moment. But his first words were not, as Sam expected, "What the hell happened to you?"

Instead, he roared, "Well, Airman! Reporting for duty?"

Sam nodded uncertainly. He could remember his own father greeting him; it had never been like this.

"What does an enlisted man do when he sees an officer?" the major said, with mock sternness.

Sam's eyes widened with a touch of panic. An *enlisted man*? Did he actually . . . ?

Apparently, he actually. Major Robicheaux shifted, subtly, and somehow he was standing at attention. Sam copied his posture, searching for any other signs, either of approval or of concern at the bruises marking his daughter's face. He couldn't find either one.

He did see a frown beginning, as if expectations weren't being fulfilled. Though he had no idea what those expectations might be.

"Salute, Sam," came Al's voice from behind him. Sam breathed a sigh of relief and brought his right hand up to his eyebrow.

"Straight hand, not cupped," Al coached. Sam flattened his hand and executed a credible salute.

"*No*," Al said with a touch of exasperation. "You're supposed to hold it until he returns the salute."

At this point Sam would have liked to ask Al some serious questions about what Navy recruiting practices consisted of—or perhaps it was Air Force recruiting that concentrated on preschoolers. But the narrowing of the major's eyes indicated that Al was probably correct, so he hastily raised his hand once again, in the approved flat arrangement, and held it to his eyebrow.

The major returned the salute in precise, academy fashion.

"Okay, Sam, finish it."

Sam snapped his arm down.

"What does an officer do when he sees a swabbie with marks like those on his face?" Al growled, having moved around from behind Sam and caught sight of Missy's face. "Good God Almighty, Sam, what happened to you? You look like somebody put you through a meat grinder!"

"Very good," Steve said. After his first reaction, he seemed to notice nothing unusual at all. "Now, aren't you going to give me a hug?"

Sam took a deep breath, stepped forward, and raised his arms. He was surprised at the enthusiasm with which the officer grabbed him and lifted him exuberantly into the air. "That's my girl!" he said. "Did you miss me?"

"Oh, yeah," Sam gasped, flailing for the ground and just missing kicking Missy's father in the Good Conduct ribbon. The feeling of being lifted completely off his feet and swung into the air was extremely disconcerting. He wondered fleetingly if any women had felt this way when he picked them up. He wondered if he had ever picked a woman up. He thought it was likely. He made a mental note to try to remember that it might not be an enjoyable experience in all cases for the pick-ee.

"I'm okay," he added for Al's benefit.

"Yes, sir," Al said warningly. "You don't say 'yeah' in this house." He shook his head. "Look like somebody already pointed that out to you. Are you sure you're all right? Did Jane do this?"

"I mean, Yes, sir," Sam corrected himself, and answered both questions at once in the most economical fashion possible. His lips hurt.

"Good girl." Sam felt a bit like a cocker spaniel puppy being praised. The major set him down again and patted him on the head. "We're going to make a real little airman out of you."

"Yeah, right," Al cracked. "Not so little, really."

153

Sam turned and glared at the Observer, careful to keep his expression out of Steve's line of sight. It made no difference. The major picked up the briefcase and walked past, as if having greeted his daughter he could now completely ignore her existence. In a few strides he arrived at the door of the master bedroom, and disappeared inside.

"What the *hell* was that all about?" Sam asked angrily. "Am I supposed to be his kid or one of his recruits?"

Al shrugged and waved his cigar in an expressive circle. "There isn't any difference, from his point of view," he said. "Discipline is discipline, right?"

Sam was incredulous. "Are you telling me you think it's *okay* to have kids *saluting* their fathers?"

Al shrugged again. "Hey, it's not my kid. And I can understand it. It's the same standard he applies to his subordinates in his command; Missy is his subordinate at home. Why should there be a difference?"

"Where's the real Al and what have you done with him?"

Al stopped and stared at him. "I said I understood, Sam, not that I approved. It's not the way you or I were brought up, but that doesn't make it immoral."

"I think it's sick!"

"Sick is what Jane's doing, not what the major wants. You're *sure* you're okay?" When Sam nodded, Al shook his head. "You never did understand the military mind." He floated over to the kitchen counter, making a show of examining the bottles lined up there. "What's this all about?"

"I was going to pour them out." Sam was still upset, but considered that there was no point in continuing the argument. He felt as if someone had argued the reasonableness of some alien custom, such as eating puppies. There was no logical reason not to, but the emotional reasons could be just as compelling. While the major really had greeted his

154

daughter with affection, the business of saluting struck Sam as bizarre.

Al was punching data into the handlink. "I wouldn't suggest trying it now. Ziggy says the major likes a drink. Maybe not as well as his wife does, but if he finds that his little girl has poured out a lot of expensive booze, she's going to find herself court-martialed."

Sam grimaced, and began to put the bottles back. He couldn't expect to Leap into people whose customs, experiences, and beliefs were just like his own. Until he could demonstrate that saluting actually damaged the child in some way, he had to accept it. Childhood customs in many places *were* bizarre, after all. In some times and places, girl children were expected to curtsy to their parents. Saluting was just another version of hello, he thought. A particularly distasteful one. But "court-martial"? Surely that was a little extreme?

He could hear voices coming from the bedroom, mostly unintelligible. There were sounds of welcome, then a reference to "chaplain contacted me" and "Jeanne," "Russians" and "readiness." Sam left the bottles and moved down the hall, trying to catch more of the discussion.

"Maybe he'll stay home and prevent everything," he said hopefully.

As he spoke, he could hear Jane saying, " . . . she keeps tripping and falling into that table . . ."

"Nope," Al said. "He's here to comfort his wife, pick up a change of uniforms, and make sure his family is ready for the alert. That's not kosher," he added disapprovingly. "They're not supposed to have any advance warning." Al stuck his hologrammic head through the door. Most, but not all, of his body followed. Sam looked away. He knew that Al wasn't physically present, but watching half a body still bothered his stomach.

"Al, quit eavesdropping," he whispered. "Come on."

The Observer stuck his head out of the door. "Oh, like you aren't standing there trying to hear something?" he said acidly. "Do you want to know what's going on or not?"

There wasn't any answer for that, either. "All right," he responded. "What's going on?"

"I don't know yet. But he's doing a pretty good job of saying hello to his wife." Al stuck his head back into the bedroom.

"Al!"

Al pulled out again, reluctantly. "What?"

"Could you exercise your voyeuristic tendencies somewhere else, please? I'm trying to accomplish something here!"

"Oh, all right." He checked the handlink, as a formality, and nodded. "Nope, nothing's changed. Daddy stays for dinner, leaves, there's a big fight, and Tom runs away."

And dies, Sam realized with a chill.

"What if he doesn't come home while his father's here?"

"Doesn't matter," Al said, querying the computer. "Whether he comes home for dinner and gets into a fight afterward, or never comes back, he still goes out and sets a fire."

"I'll bet Walt was with him," Sam muttered.

The handlink squealed. "Well, yes, as a matter of fact it looks like he might have been," Al reported, examining the data stream. "Nothing official, but somebody mentioned questioning him. I'll bet he *was* there, the little sneak."

"What happens to Walt?"

"It looks like . . . yeah, he becomes an international sales representative for one of those marginal phone companies. He ends up dying of AIDS in about twenty-five years. Contracted from a blood transfusion during some surgery he had in France in the eighties. That tainted-blood scandal."

"Ouch."

"Would you be happier if he'd died in a car wreck? He'd still be dead. Or cancer, maybe? It can take just as long to die of cancer as auto-immune deficiency."

"What is wrong with you?" Sam demanded. "I know you're cynical, but this is something else!"

"No it isn't." Al tapped on the handlink. When this met with no response, he slapped it with the flat of his hand. The machine burped and blinked as if startled.

The bedroom door opened, slicing through Al as if he wasn't there—which, in fact, was true. Sam still jumped at the sight.

The major apparently thought his daughter was suffering from guilt at being caught. "What are you doing there?" he snapped. He made no concession to the fact that he was speaking to a child. His voice was harsh, clipped.

"Nothing," Sam responded automatically. A stray memory surfaced of a book he had read once, with the engaging title *Where Did You Go? Out. What Did You Do? Nothing*. He understood the title perfectly, of a sudden.

But it didn't matter now. He stepped back, away from the towering, threatening figure.

Apparently the major decided Missy had been sufficiently intimidated, or perhaps he recognized how little it took to overwhelm a preschooler.

"Where's your brother?" he asked next.

"I don't know," Sam replied with complete honesty. He shot a glance at Al.

"I can't seem to center on Tom," Al said, frowning at the handlink. "We didn't get a good fix on him."

"He was supposed to have checked in by now," Jane said, appearing in the doorway behind the major. She was tying the fabric belt of a robe. "I can't imagine where he'd be. Missy, do you know?"

Sam shook his head.

The major checked his watch. "He's past due." Brushing by Sam, he marched into Missy's room and went to the window, opening it wide. Sam followed him just in time to see him raise his hands to his mouth as if to whistle.

Three earsplitting blasts later, the major pulled the window shut. "That will bring him."

Him, and every dog for four counties, Sam thought. But he kept quiet, following Missy's father out of the room and into the dining room. As predicted, Steve went from there into the kitchen.

"What's all this?" he said, indicating the bottles.

Sam glanced around, took a deep breath. "I was going to pour them out," he said. His voice sounded high pitched and frightened, even to himself.

"You were *what*? Why?"

"Because Mom drinks too much."

The ice blue eyes widened in shock. Then they shifted and looked up. Heart sinking, Sam turned to find Jane Robicheaux standing behind him, a red flush rising in her cheeks.

"What are you talking about?"

Feeling committed far beyond the point any child should be, Sam repeated, "Mom drinks too much. And then she hits me. So I was going to pour it out."

"Just who do you think you are!" Jane snapped, grabbing him by the shoulder and spinning him around. "How dare you say things like that! Who taught you to say things like that!"

"I'd like to know who she heard it from too," the major said grimly.

Both parents were deliberately ignoring Sam's accusation about being beaten, and were focusing on the drinking. They didn't believe their daughter could have come to the conclusion on her own, Sam realized. Missy was too young. She was still at the age where she would repeat what she heard, like a parrot. But the woman's fingers bit into his shoulder nonetheless, her fingernails making little semicircles of pain through the thin shirt.

"Who told you?" he said. "Who did you hear that from?"

"No-nobody." His voice was quavering, Sam noticed with disgust. But he couldn't seem to control it. "I just thought—"

"How *dare* you!" Jane half shrieked. Her hand left his shoulder, drew back and flashed forward to strike Missy's face with lightning speed. "How dare you talk about me that way! Your own mother!"

"She had to have heard that from somewhere," Sam heard Steve say, through a red haze of pain and blinding tears. "Unless—*Have* you been drinking again?"

Holding one hand up to his stinging face, Sam stepped away, getting out from between the two furious adults. They ignored him, squaring off as if for battle.

"Have you been drinking again?" the major repeated.

He was paying no attention to his daughter's pain, no attention at all to the evidence in front of his eyes about the source of his daughter's bruises. Sam sniffed back the tears threatening to overwhelm him—a reaction less to the pain than to the shock of the blow, he thought, interesting that it should affect a child so differently from an adult—and stepped back to watch.

"It doesn't change anything," Al said. Sam jumped. He'd completely forgotten about the Observer. Al was watching the confrontation too, tense and as angry as either of the participants. "How could she hit her kid that way?" he muttered, to himself rather than to Sam. "And he doesn't even notice!"

Sam let go of a breath he wasn't aware he was holding. The two adults were still arguing, their voices pitched low so as not to carry through the walls to any interested listeners.

"For God's sake," Jane was saying, "so I have a drink every once in a while. So do you! There's nothing wrong with it! I don't know where she gets these ideas! I do *not* get drunk!"

"I should hope you don't," the major was responding. "That's all I need right now; a wife who parades around drunk. Do you think they're going to trust me with a bigger command if I can't even keep my own house in order? Damn it, I told you to quit drinking!"

"I haven't *been* drinking like that!" she shot back.

"Then what's that smell on your breath? Mouthwash?"

"Look, I have a drink every once in a while. So does everybody else, there's nothing wrong with it!"

Sam, nursing the pain of his bruised face and shoulder, could have told her differently. Neither one of them thought to look at the little girl standing in the corner, huddled behind the Observer, who had moved in front of her to protect her, however futile the gesture might be.

"Look, things are getting hot," the major said, lowering his voice still further. Sam couldn't tell whether the man was making an effort to placate his wife, or was trying to be more intimidating. Jane was facing him with her hands balled into fists, her eyes suspiciously bright. "We have to be ready. Ready, do you understand?"

"Oh, ready." Jane laughed. It was interesting, Sam thought, that even laughter tinged with hysteria could be kept discreetly low. "Ready to duck missiles? What chance do we have if they decide to cross the border? What's the point?"

"You don't have any chance at all if you're not ready," the major said. His voice was definitely lower now. "Look, I can't leave a mess like this behind me. I only have a few hours anyway. Come on, Janey. Do we need to pour out that liquor or not?"

"Of course not!" she said. "If you think you can't depend on me—" She laughed again, a laugh that ended in a strangled sob. "It's not as if I can run home to Mother, now is it? Mother's three thousand miles away!"

Steve closed his eyes, acknowledging the change, however minor, in his wife's attitude. "Look, the chaplain said you might need me, but if you think you have things under control here—I have to get my things together. I have to eat something and get on the road again. I have some briefings. Things are getting really bad—" He caught himself and shut up quickly.

Jane picked up on the cut-off thought. "It's going to be soon, isn't it?" she whispered. Her hands relaxed, her fingers stretching as if seeking something to grasp. "It's really going to happen, isn't it?"

"We don't know that. I didn't say that," he said quickly. But it was too late, and not convincing. Something went out of her, and she seemed to shrink inside.

The immediate threat abated, Al had relaxed a little too, and the officer's words had him tapping Ziggy for data. "It's beginning," he told Sam. "They've restricted the movement of East German workers into West Berlin. Restricted, hell, they've stopped it. Sixty thousand people just lost their jobs because they lived on one side of the street and worked on the other. And they're turning the West Berliners back at Brandenburg and all the other gates. Hoenecker—that's the East German security chief, at least he is now, he'll be Premier of East Germany later on—he's stopped talking to the Allied representatives. If you had to Leap into somebody, Sam. . . ."

Sam shook his head. He was watching the Robicheauxs. They were still staring at each other, standing perhaps five feet apart, making no effort to comfort each other, as if something invisible and high separated them from each other.

161

It was Jane Robicheaux who broke the tableau. "You have to eat," she said, as if feeding her husband before he left again was the most important thing she could do. "Tom will just have to wait, if he doesn't get here in time."

Her husband didn't say anything, but only stepped aside to let her pass. Neither one of them looked at their daughter.

CHAPTER

SIXTEEN

"We will use force . . ."
—Gerhart Eisler,
East German propaganda minister

They ate dinner in silence, with quick, precise movements, chew, swallow, as if efficiency were everything. They had water glasses and wine, and Jane
drank slowly but steadily. Her cheekbones and her
eyes were bright from the alcohol, but her hands
didn't tremble.

Major Robicheaux checked his watch every few
minutes. "Where was he going?" he said at last.

Sam wasn't sure the question was directed to him,
so he kept silence, moving mashed potatoes around
the plate and guiding brown gravy through channels.
It hurt too much to open his mouth wide enough to
get food inside, much less to chew.

"I asked you a question," the major said.

Sam looked up, alarmed. The question *had* been
directed to him, after all. "Yes?"

"Yes, *sir*," Al prompted quietly from behind him.
Sam jumped, covering it by reaching for his water
glass and knocking it over. A flood of water soaked
the linen tablecloth.

"I'm sorry!" he said breathlessly, jumping up and

trying to soak up the damage.

"Sit down."

The words jerked Sam's head around as if they were string attached to his nose. The major was staring at him, his cold blue eyes expressionless. The water soaked its way to the edge of the table and began to drip to the floor. Sam sat down, carefully. Part of him was afraid of the expression in those eyes. Another part took it as a challenge. But all of him was glad that Al was at his back, hologram or not. "Yes, sir?" he said evenly.

"I asked you a question, and you haven't answered it."

Sam opened his mouth and closed it again. If he answered as Sam Beckett would have answered, they would doubtless consider their daughter possessed. The fact that she *was* possessed, at least in a manner of speaking, didn't make things easier. He had to make them think he was only a child, and at a moment like this one, he wasn't sure how.

"Say you're sorry, Sam," Al prompted from behind him. Sam could hear the soft whistles of the handlink.

"I'm sorry," he said.

He started to continue, but Al said, "No. Just keep quiet. I'll tell you what to say."

Sam shut up and waited for his next cue.

"Where's Tom?" Robicheaux repeated.

"Say, 'He went outside.' "

"He went outside."

"Don't say any more yet," Al warned. "You're six, remember. And you're scared."

"Where outside?" the major roared, leaning forward and reaching out. Sam didn't have to pretend to flinch away.

"I . . . I don't know," he stammered, before Al could coach him. "I don't know where he went."

Why was he so frightened? he wondered, even as he squirmed back in his seat. But looking at the size

164

of the angry adult relative to Missy, he knew the answer. Major Robicheaux didn't make allowances for the cognitive development of a preschool child. He had a question, and he wanted an answer.

"Tom didn't tell me where he was going," Sam said. "He just left."

"You know you're supposed to come when you're called?"

"Maybe he didn't hear." Sam was perilously close to arguing with the man, and it would only end in disaster. "He couldn't come if he didn't hear."

The clink of glass against glass, as Jane emptied a bottle of wine, distracted them both.

"Don't try to fight him," Al cautioned. But Sam already knew better than to fight, and the interruption, deliberate or not, had served to defuse the situation.

The door buzzer sounded, signaling a request for release of the downstairs entrance. "There he is," Jane said with relief. She had set aside her glass and was rubbing her temples.

The major got up and strode to the door, hitting the speaker button. "Who is it?"

"Corporal Adams," came the response, barely understandable beneath the static. "Your car, sir."

Jane made a sound of protest.

The man smothered a curse. "Stand by!"

"Yes, sir."

Major Robicheaux turned away and looked at his wife and daughter, and for a split second Sam thought he saw a gleam of fear in his eyes. "When Tom shows up," the major said, "you tell him he's confined to quarters until further notice. He knows what the rules are. He's supposed to check in every two hours, no matter what he's doing. I've been here almost five hours and we haven't heard anything. That isn't acceptable. Do you understand?"

Not sure whether the man was addressing his wife or his daughter, Sam nodded. Out of the corner of his eye, he could see Jane nodding too. Her forehead was furrowed with pain.

"I have to leave now," Robicheaux continued.

"But you just got here," his wife protested. "You only had a few hours!"

"That's all they'd give me," he said. He was addressing his wife alone this time, and once again Sam felt as if he had vanished from the room, as thoroughly as ever Al did stepping into the Door. "I have to get to . . . I have to leave, that's all."

"MAC Headquarters, I'll bet," Al said softly, still behind Sam. "He was supposed to go directly, but when the chaplain called about the death of his wife's sister, he got permission to stop off to see his family while he had the chance. Shame the kid wasn't here."

Evidently the major thought so too, but looked at it differently. "Tell Tom he's going to have to answer to me," he said. He went back into the master bedroom, returned with a briefcase and his uniform jacket, and came over to the table where Jane still sat. "You tell him that," he said, as if he had never left the room.

"I'll tell him," she said.

"And you—" he turned to Sam—"I don't want to hear another word out of you about drinking, understand? That subject is off limits. Period."

"Yes, sir." Sam wondered if the man had noticed who had consumed most of the wine with dinner. He probably had. But no official notice was being taken, and therefore, it never happened. Just as no official notice was being taken of the damage to Missy's face.

"I want you to obey your mother, you understand? When I'm gone, she's in charge. No arguments. Don't give her any problems."

"Yes, sir." It was almost like a change-of-command ceremony, he thought, fascinated, except that American commanders rarely transferred their commands with a quick kiss on the lips. It took Jane by surprise, too. She tried to smile at her husband, but it was too difficult.

The major took a deep breath and looked around him, as if trying to remember something important. But nothing recommended itself to his attention, and he nodded, sharply. "All right. I'll be back . . . as soon as I can. Remember what I told you, Jane. It's important. And get Tom back here, understand? We can't have him running off any old time."

"Yes, dear," she murmured, the words aggravating what was clearly a large headache.

The door closed behind her husband, leaving her alone in the apartment with Sam.

"My head hurts," she murmured, and went back to the dining room table. There was still a half glass of wine at her husband's place. She picked it up and drained it, moved around to her own place at the opposite end, picked up her own glass, and noticed that it was empty. So was the bottle. She took the glass into the kitchen.

Sam followed her. "Please don't do that," he said, as she took up another bottle of wine and unwrapped the foil.

Jane made a wobbly turn and looked at him. "Don't do what?"

"Please don't drink any more."

She raised her eyebrows, viewing her daughter and the bottle in her hand. "This? This is just because Mommy has a little headache, honey. This isn't really a drink." Her eyebrows squeezed together. "Besides, didn't you hear what Daddy said? You're not supposed to talk about Mommy having a drink. Not ever."

She was sober enough, still, to work the cork out of the bottle, even if she did a bad job of it. Sam looked desperately to Al for some ideas, some suggestions, some encouragement, something. Al shook his head.

"I don't know, Sam. Ziggy says she died from pills and alcohol. I don't know about the pills, but she's certainly doing a good job with the alcohol."

"Maybe I can do something about the pills, then," Sam said.

"What did you say?" Jane asked, clicking the lip of the bottle against the crystal.

"Nothing." *What did you do? Nothing. . . .*

He slipped away, leaving Jane behind him topping off the glass. Al floated after, giving the woman a wide berth and a pitying glance.

"Now what?" the Observer asked. "She's drinking, and we don't know where Tom is. You know, you could have picked somebody a little more—*proactive*—to Leap into this time. What can a little girl do, after all?"

"It wasn't exactly my decision," Sam said, going into the bathroom and climbing up on the toilet and, from there, to the sink, where he knelt precariously, hanging on to the edge of the mirrored cabinet door.

"Will you look at that!" Al said. The cabinet was fairly stuffed with small brown plastic bottles labeled in white.

"Miltown—Valium—look at this. Every prescription by a different doctor. What's she doing, going doctor shopping?"

"Military medical," Al said. "No such thing as a regular doctor. You see whoever's there. By the time you go in again, he's been transferred. Sometimes they don't bother to go through the medical records, just give the patient what he asks for."

"Is that medicine?" Sam said, outraged.

Al shrugged. "It is in the military. Oh, there are good doctors too. You just don't get to choose."

"It's obscene." He began to take bottles out and put them on the sink, two at a time. By the time he had them all on the sink, three had fallen on the floor.

Sliding down was easier than getting up. He had just poured the contents of the first bottle into the toilet when voices from the living room caught Al's attention. The hologram ducked out to see what was going on. Seconds later, he was back.

"It's Tom. He's home. You'd better get out here, Sam."

Tom was late and unrepentant. He was startled, though, at the sight of the dining room table.

"You already had dinner," he said. "You had dinner without me."

"Where were you? You were supposed to be home hours ago. You were supposed to check in." Sam could hear the hint of shrillness in her tone that warned of a potential explosion, and he prepared to duck.

Tom shook his head, more as if to dislodge an annoying fly than to deny anything, and took a piece of bread.

Jane snatched the food out of his hand.

"Oh, no," Al groaned. "That does it."

"Your father was here, and you didn't check in! You were supposed to check in! You're confined to quarters, do you understand me?" She was leaning over, her face only inches from his. "We have to know where you are all the time!"

"I was just out playing!" Tom didn't know whether he should be frightened or angry. The smell of wine on the woman's breath was almost overwhelming, even to Sam, a few steps away. "I came home for dinner!"

"Your father was here for dinner!" she screamed at him. "Your father was here and you weren't home! He called you and you didn't come! Where were you? You lazy, useless, disobedient boy! You don't deserve to have a father! You don't deserve to have a family!"

"Daddy came home?" Tom was looking at Sam now, shocked. "He was really here?"

169

Sam nodded. He was trying to keep an eye on both of them at once, though he wasn't sure what he could do. Jane straightened unevenly, the slice of bread still in her hand. "Go to your room and stay there," she said carefully. "Don't come out until I tell you to."

Sam could see Tom still looking at the bread, and realized the boy was hungry. He wished there was some way he could tell Tom that he would sneak him some food later, if he'd only go obediently to his room and not argue now.

For a moment it almost looked as if the boy would go. Jane stepped back toward the table, taking her glass again. She realized that she was still holding the bread and looked at her hands, as if confused about which one she should put down and which one she should drink.

Tom snorted and went for an apple from the centerpiece bowl of fruit.

Bread and wine went crashing to the floor as his mother slapped at him. "Dammit, I told you to go to your room! I want you to do what you're told! Can't you ever do what you're told?"

Both Tom and Sam stepped back involuntarily. Jane's eyes were black with fury, her hair was sticking out at odd angles, red patches stood out against her pale skin. "Go on!"

Tom retreated, step by step, and she followed, backing him literally down the hall and into his room, her hand raised, ready to strike. "Don't you ever do what you're told!"

"Don't you hit him," Al yelled, furious. "Don't hit him. He hasn't done anything." But Jane couldn't see him, and Sam couldn't respond to him, as much as he might want to, as much as he agreed with the Observer's anger.

"I just wanted to get something to eat!" Tom finally yelled, pushed beyond endurance. "What are you going to do, starve me?"

Jane lashed out, knocking the boy into the dresser. Reaching out to catch himself, he clutched at the half-finished model, and it crumpled in his hands. Seeing it, feeling the destruction, he shrieked and threw it at his mother.

She shrieked back and knocked a whole series of completed models off the table in the process of reaching for him. "Don't you talk back to me! Damn you, don't you talk back to me! You little ungrateful monster! Monster!"

Tom dodged, half falling over the knapsack propped beside the bed. Sam watched, sick, as the boy's fingers closed over the strap and he came up swinging. The knapsack caught his mother in the face, and she staggered, catching herself on the dresser. "Tom!" she screamed.

But it was too late. Tom was out the door, knapsack in hand, and Jane and Sam and Al could all hear the front door slamming behind him.

"There he goes," Al said gloomily. *"Nothing's* going right this Leap."

"Oh my God," she moaned, sliding down the wall to sit on the floor. One hand covered her left eye, and she curled up into herself, moaning.

"Are you hurt?" Sam asked, coming over to examine her. The buckle on the strap had caught her above the eye, and blood was beginning to well up. "You need to put some ice on that right away."

"My little nurse," she mumbled. "Take care of Mommy. Mommy needs her little nurse. Mommy needs *somebody.* . . . Oh, please, somebody, take care of Mommy. Somebody. . . ." She burst into tears.

"I'll get the ice," Sam said. "Don't move."

"She doesn't look like she *can* move," Al said. "She's half out of it." He followed Sam out to the kitchen, watched as he scrambled into the small freezer compartment for ice cubes, broke them out of the tray and wrapped them into a rough linen towel. "Going to be a nurse, huh?"

"I'm not a nurse, I'm a doctor," Sam said. "And she ought to see a doctor about that cut."

"You're six," Al said. "You're a girl. Of course you're going to be a nurse. That's what girls do."

Sam shot him a look that should have melted the ice by sheer radiant heat. Al smirked and raised his hands in mock surrender. The return to the bedroom erased any trace of levity. "Ooooh, she looks bad," he said, whispering in sympathy, even though Jane couldn't hear him.

Sam had to agree. She was slumped into the corner formed by the dresser and the wall, blood welling around the hand pressed to her forehead and trickling down her wrist to stain the cuff of her white blouse, sobbing quietly amid the ruins of the toy airplanes. Sam moved her hand away, meeting no resistance, and pressed the package of ice to her forehead.

She whimpered and tried to flinch away, without success. Sam held her hand away and applied the ice to the rapidly swelling and blackening cut. "It's okay," he said. "It's okay, please don't cry."

After a moment she took the ice herself. "That's so cold," she said, trying to smile.

"It's ice, it's supposed to be cold," Sam said.

"Where did Tom go?"

"He ran away," Sam said with a sudden chill. "He . . . ran away."

The tentative smile vanished. "Oh, God, it never goes right. Nothing I do ever goes right. . . ."

As if in agreement, in the distance, sirens began to wail.

CHAPTER
SEVENTEEN

"The borders of the German Democratic Republic must, if necessary, be defended militarily . . . the war hysteria ignited in West Germany is madness. . . ."   —Walter Ulbricht

Al, caught by surprise, dropped his cigar. It vanished as soon as it left his hand. "What is it?" Sam asked sharply.

"I don't know whether it's a drill or the real thing," he said. "I don't know which history we're in any more. Things are too different."

The sound of the sirens—the rising and falling blast that was not happening at Monday noon for test purposes, was not stopping after only one minute—finally penetrated to Jane. "Oh my God," she whispered. "That's it. That's it, the alert. Where's . . . ?" She tried to get to her feet, pulling herself up by the edge of the dresser, and slipped back again to her knees. "We have . . . we don't have any time. Tom—where's Tom? We have to go! We have to find Tom!" She couldn't get up. "Tom? Steve?"

"Is the major going to come back to get them?" Sam asked Al as he tried to support her.

Jane heard only part of the sentence, the part she thought made sense. "Steve? Come back?" Despite herself, she laughed.

"No way," Al said firmly. "He's at battle stations, or whatever the Air Force types call it. He can't come back. She has to get the family together and evacuate. She's got two hours to have the kids and all their stuff together and get on the road, Sam. That's it."

"But Tom's gone—"

"Tom's gone for a date with a fire," Al reminded him. "And she's in no shape to help. You have to find him."

"You have to find him," Jane repeated, in an eerie echo. "Find Tom. Bring him home. I'm . . . going to take care of things."

Al swiveled his head around at her tone. "Oh no. She's going to take the pills—Sam, you can't leave her."

They could hear voices in the stairwell as the neighbors across the landing came out of the apartment. "I could ask the people across the way to stay—" Sam began.

"They're not going to stay for her," Al said. "They're leaving."

"No," Jane said at the same time. "Go on. Go get Tom, honey, we don't have much time." She shifted to her knees, struggled to get up.

"No, please," Sam said. "Stay quiet, please. I'll get Tom. Just stay here, please? Promise?"

Jane tried to smile. "Okay, honey, I promise."

Sam shot a desperate glance at the Observer, who was reading the data feed from the handlink and shaking his head. Nothing had changed. Promise or no promise, the woman would die. Unless he got rid of the pills. He got up and dashed to the bathroom, snatched up bottles and dumped them as fast as he could, his ears ringing to the sounds of the sirens wailing and the echoing voices in the stairwells, the

174

crashes and slams of people running down steps while carrying bags and suitcases, children crying, women shouting. Flushing the toilet repeatedly, he barely waited to see if the pills went swirling away before he left to check again on Jane.

"Sam, you've got to hurry," Al warned unnecessarily.

She was still sitting on the floor, wiping gingerly at the cut on her forehead. "Missy? Missy, what are you doing here? You're supposed to find Tom!" She tried to get up, held her hand to her mouth as the movement nauseated her. "Missy, please!"

"I'm going," Sam said. "I'll find him. It'll be okay. Really."

He hoped it would be okay, but for the life of him he couldn't see how.

The stairwell was empty, the other occupants of the apartments gone already. Sam raced down six half-flights and reached for the front door, then stopped, still in the little vestibule of the first floor. "Al? Where am I going?"

Al, not bound to mere stairs, floated straight down from the third floor to the first, studying the handlink. "You've gotta find the kid," he started.

"I *know* that." Sam reached for the door and stopped again. "I don't know where to look. I don't know where to start. I don't know where Tom hangs out, or—"

"Where he plays," Al corrected. "He won't start hanging out for oh, a few years yet." He shook his head. "He's found in a utility shed, but we don't know which one—"

"Would Missy know?"

Al shrugged. "Would your little sister know, when you were that age? Ten years old, you don't want your kid sister tagging around after you. You spend a lot of time trying to keep your life private."

"If Missy is anything like Katie was, she knows everything about him anyway. I'm going to look in

175

the basement and over by the playground, just in case; go talk to Missy, okay? See if she knows anything."

Al studied him a moment, and then his gaze drifted downward to the handlink, as if he were reluctant to use it. But without further comment, he punched in the proper code, and the Door opened. He punched the handlink again, and the Door dropped shut, and Sam was alone.

The laundry room was still paneled in sheets and underwear. The fabric muffled the repeated wails of the sirens. Sam paused at the door. "Tom! Are you in there?"

There wasn't any answer. But if Tom were there, ignoring the evacuation signal, he wouldn't answer a call from his little sister either, so Sam moved down one side of the room, looking down the tunnels made by line after line of laundry. There was no one else in the room.

All the doors to the maids' quarters were shut. Behind one of them Sam could hear women sobbing and praying in German, something about the Russians coming, and rapes, and Berlin. He listened for a moment, feeling sick at the waves of fear coming through the closed door. There would be no room for the German maids in the evacuation of American dependents. They would be left behind, defenseless, to meet the invaders. If there were any invaders. If there was anything left to invade, once the bombs fell. . . .

Tom wouldn't be there. Sam moved on, trying the doors behind which silence waited. Some were locked. One, Marta's, was open; the room was empty.

The storage cages were still filled with goods and empty of humanity.

He took the steps back up two at a time and went outside. The sun was setting. Only one car, the Robicheauxs' car, was parked in front of the building. It had been perhaps thirty minutes since the sirens first sounded, and Texasstrasse was empty. All the families, well trained to fear, had grabbed the packed suitcases waiting by their respective front doors and vanished as if in smoke.

Sam saw a movement in the hedge dividing Missy's apartment block from the next one down and ran to see. It was the German shepherd, still muzzled, a red leash hanging from its collar. The dog paused to look at him and growled softly. Sam kept very still and counted to himself. Eighteen seconds later, the dog whined and slunk away, looking for its missing master, dragging the leash behind itself. Sam turned and ran toward the playground. He could hear traffic somewhere, far away, but he couldn't see anyone, anywhere. Hainerberg had become a ghost town, as if the smoke from the red flares had dissolved everything human it had touched. In the distance, he could hear the rapidly receding sound of automobile engines as dependents fled.

The siren still beat at his ears as he scanned the swings, the sandbox where Tom and Walt had played with matches only a day ago. Walt—where did Walt live? Would Tom be with Walt? He wished Al would get back with some more information. The playground was empty too. One of the swings moved back and forth, gently, as if recently abandoned. It was as if the occupant—as well as the rest of the several thousand people living in the housing complex—had "bailed out" of the swing and the artificial town itself to flee to some imagined safety, out of range of the missiles and tanks swiveling to aim Westward into their front windows.

He didn't know where Walt lived. But he could keep looking, at least, knowing that no matter how far he went or how lost he got, Al would find him and make sure he got back in time. At least now, with the pills gone, he could worry less about Jane. All he had to do now was find Tom before it was too late.

Through the chain-link and berrybush playground boundary he could see a sedan go by, moving slowly, almost prowling. It was marked with the insignia of the Military Police. Probably to keep looters from moving in, he thought. There would probably be opportunists willing to take advantage of the mass abandonment of the complex.

He considered briefly the possibility of enlisting the MPs in the search for Tom, and decided against it, at least until he found out what Al had to say. If he tried to explain, they'd be as likely as not to pick him up and bundle him off to an evacuation rendezvous without bothering to listen. To them, after all, he was a little girl, too young yet to be in the first grade, out alone. They'd assume her family had left without her. It was their job to pick up stragglers.

Maybe they'd picked up Tom. He cherished the thought for at least a minute and a half before reluctantly abandoning it. If Tom was safe, Al would have come back to tell him, or he would have Leaped. Since neither event had occurred, he had to assume that Tom was still doomed until he managed to find him and change history.

Trotting down the length of the playground, he left through the gate at the far end. Before him, a series of apartment buildings, identical to the one in which the Robicheaux family lived except for the numbers painted by the stairwells, rose up in an orderly file. He couldn't see anyone on the lawn stretching from the front of the building to the street, so he swung around to follow the back line.

There were external entrances to the basements, he noticed, with a single flight of stairs stretching down. A low shed was attached to the back of each building, too. He paused to look at the first one, but the door was padlocked shut. There wasn't anyone there. He kept going, puffing to himself, calling out when he dared. There was no one to answer.

Hainerberg seemed to be empty of everything but sirens and one small figure, doggedly searching.

The image of the stairwell blinked out as Al lifted his finger from the handlink the last time, and he was standing in the Imaging Chamber again, in the cold blue-white light that pervaded the Project. He blinked and shook his head, adjusting to the abrupt change.

"Ziggy?" His voice sounded tight, even to himself. It felt tight, too.

"Yes, Admiral." Ziggy's voice was a little less brisk and businesslike than usual, he thought.

"What's changed?"

If the computer could sigh, it would have. In the event, a soft burr of static served instead. "Nothing substantial has changed since you entered the Chamber, Admiral. Tina and Gushie are still married. Dr. Beeks is in her quarters. She has asked to be notified when you return."

Al blinked again, keeping his eyes closed a little longer this time. He ought to be used to it by now. Lord knows he'd gone through it often enough.

He took a deep breath. The best he could hope for was that when Sam finally got back home, the timestream he returned to, the one that would remain fixed, would be the one Al wanted most. But there were no guarantees in this life. None.

Right now, there were more important things to worry about than his love life. Not many, perhaps, but at least two: Tom and Jane's lives. "Ziggy, tell Verbeena we need to get some information from Missy right away. Ask her to meet me in the Waiting Room."

"Are you planning to go there directly?" Ziggy asked. At the same time, Al knew, the request was being transmitted to Verbeena. He wasn't sure how many people in the Project Ziggy could talk to at

179

one time, or how many simultaneous conversations the computer could carry on; it didn't matter, really, but it did tend to cut down on communications lag, which was nice.

The computer could probably transmit voices, too, but they had never tried that particular experiment. Al was rather glad of that. He suspected Sam had arranged to have his own unique sense of prudishness programmed in, and Al didn't want to find some of his more intimate encounters broadcast all over the Project as a combined practical joke and lesson in morality.

He exited the airlock and strode down the ramp. The techs at the control table, a larger version of the handlink, nodded as he went by. They used to look at him eagerly every time he came out, hoping that he'd have word that the Director had made it back. Now they simply nodded greetings at him. Nobody expected good news these days. The Director was simply gone, and no one knew when or if he would ever get home again.

The door to the Waiting Room, beyond the Control Room, unlatched as he approached. Ziggy had informed the observer on duty and opened the door for him. No one had warned Missy, though, and she jerked around in her chair, startled, as he came in the room and waved an abstract greeting to the aide in the observation booth. She was sitting at a worktable, intent upon a new coloring book, and the movement caused crayons to spill across the floor in a spatter of colors.

"Hello, Missy," he said. "How are you doing today?"

"Hello," she responded, standing up and facing him. "I'm fine."

"Good." He looked around for some place to put his unlit cigar, failed to find an ashtray, and stuck it in the inner coat pocket he'd had lined for the purpose. He hated getting tobacco in the fabric of his good coats. "Missy, I need to talk to you about your brother."

The brown eyes darkened as the pupils dilated. "My brother? Is he here?"

"No, sweetheart, he isn't here. He's at home. At least, he used to be home, but he's run away. Did he talk to you about running away? Did he ever say to you that he wanted to run away? Can you remember?"

It was too much, too fast. Missy looked stunned. "Tom ran away? Is he here too?"

"No. We don't know where he is. He's lost. We need your help to find him. Please, Missy, you have to be a big girl now. Help us."

CHAPTER EIGHTEEN

"For 2,200,000 people they will declare war, and hundreds of millions of people will perish. . . ."
—Nikita Khrushchev

Too much, too fast, and just as he realized it Verbeena entered, tossing him a terrifying look as she moved to envelope Missy, who had collapsed to the floor, crying. She was dressed in a red-and-orange velveteen caftan and looked like a swirl of flame.

"Al, what are you doing here?" Verbeena knelt beside Missy and glared up at him. "What did you say to her?"

"Didn't Ziggy explain? I've got to get some information, *right now*. The alert went off, and they're evacuating, and Tom's. . . ." Abruptly, he realized that Missy was listening. She was only six, but even a six-year-old in Hainerberg knew that "alert" and "evacuating" meant Something Very Very Bad had happened.

"Tom ran away," he went on, facing Missy now and speaking directly to her. He had to think of the person in front of him as Missy; his mind, linked to Sam's, refused to recognize the physical body in front of him as Sam, even though his eyes told him clearly that that was who it was. But still it was a bit of an adjustment to see the little movements of hands and eyes and head and body and see "man" and think "child." "Where would Tom go when he ran away?"

Verbeena was trying to comfort the girl, her arms around her. "Honey, do you understand what Al wants to know?"

"He wants to know where Tom is," she said, drawing back into the shelter of the doctor's caftan-winged arms.

"That's right," Verbeena said. "Can you tell us where he might go? We really need to know, lambkin. It's very important." She was talking softly but firmly, not so much coaxing as ordering, stroking the brown hair with the wisp of white at the left temple. "Please tell us now."

"I don't know," Missy said, predictably. She wouldn't meet Al's eyes, hiding against Verbeena's arm.

Al regarded Sam Beckett in the doctor's arms, nuzzling into the silky material, and felt ill. He wanted Sam *back*, damn it all. Nothing against the kid, and it would be okay if she got back to her own body, too, but he didn't want to see his best friend acting like somebody else any more. Especially when the "somebody else" was only six.

"Didn't you ever follow Tom around to see what he did and where he went?" he asked. "Where did he like to play?"

Verbeena shook her head warningly. "Too many questions, Al. She's scared. One thing at a time."

Al took a breath to tell her that there wasn't time for "scared," but the look on Verbeena's face said that she wasn't having any of that. He pulled in a deep breath, let it out slowly, and said, "Missy, did you ever follow Tom around when he played?"

"No." The words were muffled.

"Missy, when Tom goes out to play, where does he go?" Verbeena asked. She moved her away from her sheltering shoulder, turned her to face Al. Her hands rested on the broad shoulders, keeping Missy turned away from herself. The child craned her head around to answer her.

"He likes to go to the shed."

"Where's the shed?" Al snapped. "Which shed?" Missy shrank away.

The look Verbeena gave him warned him that he was treading on thin ice indeed. He throttled back his impatience as the doctor kneaded the muscles under her hands, soothing. "It's okay, honey. Al's not mad at you, really. He just doesn't know what shed you mean. Could you tell us a little more?"

"The shed with the wood in it," the child said, still talking to Verbeena rather than to Al.

"Is it close to where you live?" the doctor coaxed.

"It's by my house."

"She may be referring to the storage shed behind the building," Ziggy commented. Missy jumped, looking for the owner of the new voice. An aerial photograph of Hainerberg blinked into existence on the east wall of the Waiting Room, taking up the entire wall with a grainy, black-and-white image of large buildings and half-grown trees.

"Oh!" Missy exclaimed. "Television!"

"The Robicheaux family lives at this address," Ziggy went on. The photo on the wall became even grainier as it blinked, sized, narrowed on one building, and expanded until the image of a single, three-story building—or at least its roof—took up most of the wall. "This is a photograph taken by a reconnaissance flight less than a year before the period of interest."

"Ziggy, you know you're not supposed to talk in the Waiting Room," Verbeena scolded.

185

"An immediate resolution is required," Ziggy responded. "Sometimes rules are meant to be broken, Doctor."

"Who is that lady who's talking?" Missy whispered, tugging at the sleeve of the caftan. "Where is she?"

"She's in another room, child. Hush now." There were no visible speakers in the Waiting Room, so Verbeena had to direct her comments to the ceiling. "I would appreciate it if you would consult me before breaking rules related to the mental health of our visitors, Ziggy. In fact, I am asking the Admiral as senior Project management to ensure that you are reprogrammed in such a way as to prevent you from doing so. The potential consequences. . . ."

Al blinked. "You're asking me to—"

"I am," Verbeena said firmly. "I will not permit my professional responsibilities to be taken over by a computer, however unique. Do I make myself clear?"

"Oh, yeah, very clear." Al rolled his eyes. "But considering the current situation, Doctor—" he hoped that his use of her title would assure Verbeena that he got the message—"don't you think that we could let Missy show us what she's talking about on the, er, television?"

"I object," Ziggy said. "I was deliberately programmed for and intended to exercise volition. Dr. Beeks's request is in direct contradiction of the aims of the original Project."

The aims of the original Project. Al wondered if that was supposed to be a not-too-subtle hint from Ziggy to himself that to tinker with Ziggy's volitional programming might very well have more far-reaching effects than anyone besides Al could suspect.

"Of course," the computer continued, "if you don't *want* me to provide input to the problem—" The picture on the wall blinked out.

Missy made a nearly inaudible sound of protest.

186

Al raised an eyebrow at the doctor. "Well, Doctor?"

She gave a small sigh of exasperation. "Of course we want your input, Ziggy. Please restore the picture."

There was a significant pause, as if Ziggy was considering human options, and Missy said, "Where's the television?"

The image blinked back on, a severely foreshortened view of the building and surrounding area, including the playground and part of the next building. Minute blurry figures represented children playing. Longer white streaks were cars moving along the street in front of the building.

"Do you know what that place is, Missy?" Al said, gesturing to the wall.

"Television," she said. Getting up, she went over to the east wall and reached up to the images up on the wall, stretching high to brush the circle of the sandbox with long fingers. For a moment, watching, Al saw the image of a young Sam Beckett, arching high to shoot a basketball straight and true into the basket.

"That's your playground, Missy," Al said. "That's your sandbox. They took the picture from an airplane, way up high. Can you see the swings?"

The hand drifted down and to the left.

"That's right. Those are the swings. Those are probably kids on the swings. It might even be you in the picture."

Missy looked back at him, uncertainly.

"You can't tell who it is, but that's okay." He took a deep breath. "Now, Missy, can you show us where the shed is where Tom likes to play?"

She studied the photograph again, from one corner to another. "It isn't here," she said at last. "I can't see it."

"Ziggy, expand the scope, please."

The photograph jumped and refocused, now revealing several buildings. Finer details, such as children in the playground, became mere dots.

"Can you find it now?"

"Is this my house?" she asked, touching the image below the playground.

"Yes, that's it." Al held his breath.

"This is it, I think." The long fingers brushed a smudge at the back of 21-19-17 Texasstrasse, at the end of the building containing the Robicheaux's stairwell, at the far end from the playground.

The photo jumped again under the hand, and she squealed and laughed in surprise. The focus now was on the smudge. Even with the specific highlight, the graininess of the image showed only a dark brown rectangle.

"Is there any other place Tom likes to play?" Al asked, trusting that Ziggy would have the volition, if not the common sense, to record the exact coordinates of the shed in memory. Still, if there were any other possibilities, they might as well identify them now. He could tell that he was going to have to have a long talk with Verbeena when this Leap was over—the doctor had quite a few ruffled feathers that needed smoothing over.

"Walt's shed," Missy replied. "He likes to go play with Walt." There was the slightest possible hesitation when she mentioned the name. Al made a mental note of it. He would have to ask Sam if there was any meaning to it. And Ziggy, who was being suspiciously silent. The computer had undoubtedly scanned its banks for the name "Walt" among all American dependents resident in Wiesbaden in 1961, and narrowed down the identity to a specific individual, already; it might even be able to speculate about the reason for the hesitation.

It might be relevant, after all.

"Where is Walt's shed?"

"By Walt's house."

Al shrugged. "Well, that makes sense."

"I have the location," Ziggy said. "Admiral. . . ."

"On my way." Al headed for the door.

"Where'd it go?" Missy said, the disappointment in her voice almost overwhelming. "Where's television?"

Al paused. "Verbeena, couldn't Ziggy show her something? *'Captain Planet'* or something?"

" *'Captain Kangaroo,'* perhaps," Ziggy said firmly. "It's from that period."

Missy lit up. "Please?"

Verbeena closed her eyes, shook her head, and gave up. "All right, she can watch *'Captain Kangaroo.'* Although—"she shot daggers at Al—"I don't see why she'd want to, since she has Mr. Green Jeans right here."

"I can't stay," Al said hastily, and headed for the door again.

Sam was panting as he jogged at a slow, steady pace down the sidewalk. He wasn't sure how many buildings he had circled, tried, and failed to enter. He wanted Al. He wanted Ziggy.

He wanted to find someone, anyone alive in Hainerberg. He had seen the MPs patrolling, and hidden until they had gone by; but other than the weeping maid, he had heard no human voices since he left the apartment. In one place someone had left a record player going, playing Elvis Presley, and for a few minutes he had hoped there was someone else left. But as he punched at the buttons, the record had begun to skip, and no one came to pick up the needle.

He sagged against the doorway. Tom was around somewhere, he had to—

"Okay, Sam, got something—"

"Where have you *been*?" Sam gasped.

"Getting information," Al said. "Okay, there are two possibilities, sheds where Missy says Tom plays.

189

One by their building, and another by Walt's—"

"That's it," Sam said with gut certainty. "Walt's. Where is it?"

"Two buildings over," Al said, orienting on the handlink and pointing with the cigar in a generally northerly direction. "In that direction."

"It figures," Sam muttered, and took off again. "Are you sure . . . you can't . . . center on . . . Tom?"

"I'm sure," Al said, floating serenely beside him. "Boy, it sure is quiet. These people took getting the hell out of here seriously, didn't they?"

Sam nodded without speaking and kept going. As he rounded the second building, he slowed to a walk, holding a hand to his ribs.

"What's the matter? Out of shape?" Al asked, too innocently. Sam glared. "Okay, okay. Missy says that Tom likes to hang out in the shed, so that would be—" He started to point again, and fell silent as Sam waved his hand in a "shushing" motion. Not that anyone else could hear Al—

The shed was not large, perhaps five feet high and six feet long and four feet wide. It was made of brownish black wooden planks, and had an ill-fitted door with a broken lock. It was the sort of place that a ten-year-old boy would look at and visualize with a "no Gurls Alowed" sign featured prominently on the outside.

There were no voices, but there was a scent in the air, and the faint crackling sound of flames. Sam moved up on the shed, peering through a gap between door and frame. "He's there, I can see him moving around. He's got a nice little campfire going." He had the feeling that the upcoming confrontation was going to be rather unpleasant. "Why don't you go and check on Jane?"

"You could call in the MPs now," Al suggested, finger hovering over the handlink. "Have them pick up our little pyromaniac here, and tell them that Mrs. R is still at home. Sew everything up nice and neat, and Leap right out of here."

Sam took a breath to argue, and stopped. He could do exactly that, and what would be the consequences? If he Leaped, at least he'd have the satisfaction of knowing he'd done what he was supposed to do. Of course, the major's career would probably be ruined . . . if the point of this Leap was to save the whole family, he had to try to find a way to do it without attracting undue attention from the military establishment. He moved uncertainly toward the street, keeping one eye on the flames in the little shed.

"Except, of course," Al went on, stopping him in his tracks, "there's never a cop around when you need one."

"Thanks a *lot*." It was true; the prowling MPs were nowhere to be seen. He craned his neck to see as far up the street as possible; there was nothing. He strained to listen. He could hear the crackling of flames, the siren. But no traffic.

"Anytime." The moving finger descended, and having descended, moved on, taking Al with it.

" 'Any*time*' my . . . oh, never mind," Sam muttered. "Tom!"

No answer.

"Tom!"

No answer.

The flames were louder. Sam took hold of the broken hasp of the door, pulling it open. Tom was sitting against the far wall of the shed, huddled with his arms around his knees. The inrush of air caused the fire before him to leap up, sending waves of heat ahead of them. Sweat began to roll into Sam's eyes.

Sam glanced around the inside of the shed and mentally cringed. The fire was fed on odd sticks and bits of scrap wood and rolled-up paper. Next to Tom were more papers, more wood, and what looked like empty paint cans and drop cloths. The place was a funeral pyre waiting to happen.

"Tom?" he called again. The boy didn't move. Sam edged around the fire. It was almost exactly in the center of the floor space, hot enough to singe as he tried to avoid the splinters. He tripped on a two-by-four, caught himself on the wall, looked down to see a colony of glossy earwigs dislodged from beneath the plank scurrying away from the heat, their mandibles opening and closing.

Tom still didn't move. As Sam approached, he tightened up, hugging himself tighter.

"Tom?" Sam said, casting an anxious glance at the fire. "Tom, didn't you hear the sirens? We have to go. It's an alert."

"I don't care," came the muffled response. "Let them come."

"Tom, come on." Greatly daring, Sam reached for one arm and tugged. "Come *on*! We've got to get out of here!"

Tom shrugged away. "No. I don't want to go back." He raised his head and looked at his sister. "I hate her. She broke my plane. She hates me. She hates you too. I hope she dies. I hope we all die."

With a sudden chill, Sam realized that Tom was speaking the simple truth. He stepped away, closer to the fire, and tripped over the plank again.

His yelp of panic broke Tom out of his paralysis, and he lunged to catch Sam as he flailed. The movement knocked the end of the plank into the fire, scattering it. The flames licked at the cloth against the wall, and caught. Tom screamed as he stepped on a coal. In twisting away from the flames, Sam put out his left arm to catch himself, got tangled, and heard the *crack* as board and bone broke together.

It was as if the scream had summoned oxygen and Al at the same moment. To Sam's eyes, Al appeared as if out of the flames, shouting, "Sam! You've got to get back—she found some more pills, she—" The

Observer took the time to look around, and said, "Sam! *Get out of here!*"

"I'm trying," Sam gasped. He picked himself up and grabbed at Tom. "Come on!" he yelled, tugging with his good hand.

Al ducked out again. Sam pulled at Tom. The flames hit the paint cans, gulped them down, and roared. Tom screamed again.

Once again, Al appeared. "There are MPs down the street, Sam. They're coming—can you get him out?"

Sam kicked at a burning mass of twigs and paper, frantic to get away from the heat and the noise and the horror. Tom twisted and struggled to get away, but he was moving to the back of the shed, not the front, and Sam had to go around him and push him through the line of what used to be a campfire.

They burst out, finally, as the fire roared up behind them. Above the moaning of the evacuation siren came a new note, as if the siren was being answered by another of its kind. Tom was crying. So was Sam.

Al wasn't. He was frantically punching data into the handlink and beating on it, frustrated, trying to read the results. "Sam, you have to get back. She found some pills, she's taken them, she's out and I think . . . Ziggy says she dies and Tom gets arrested by the MPs, everything goes to hell. Sam—get the kid away—"

"Go check on her again," Sam gasped, and pulled Tom toward the end of the building. The shed was consumed by flames now, and they were beginning to lick up the side of the building. Sam wondered if every shed was the same kind of firetrap. It seemed likely.

Tom was limping, slowing them down; Sam slowed down too, hugging his left arm to himself, glad of the chance to catch his breath again. "Are you okay?" he asked.

"Yeah," Tom said. "Are the MPs coming?"

"Yes." Sam looked back. They were standing in the shelter of a young oak tree, hidden from the activity around the shed by a low bush. "They've got a fire truck."

"A real one?"

Sam shook his head. "A real one. But if you go to look, they're going to know you set that fire, and you're going to be in *lots* of trouble."

"How could they know?"

"Because you have black marks on your face, and you have burns on your arms, and you're limping," Sam pointed out. "It won't be too hard to figure out."

Tom inspected the red marks on his arms and regarded him with amazement. "How did you get so smart?"

Sam shook his head. "We have to get home. Come on."

"I don't want to go home." Tom pulled back. "Mom's there."

Sam took a deep breath. "Yes, she is. And she's sick. She's really, really sick, Tom, and the only way we can help her is to go home. Right now. It's not her fault she's the way she is. She doesn't want to hurt us."

"But she does anyway."

Sam couldn't find an answer for that one. Tom couldn't understand a complicated psychological explanation, even if Sam had all the answers, which he most definitely did not. What it came down to, from the point of view of both Tom and Missy, was simple: Mom hurts us. Mother means pain. He couldn't find a good reason to ask Tom to go back to that.

But if he was going to keep Tom from being caught by the military police, he had to bring him along, and—

"She's getting pale, Sam, and I don't like her breathing."

It was Al, and it was bad news. Sam made a decision.

"I'm going to go home anyway," he said. "She needs me. She's sick, and somebody has to call the doctor."

"You can't do that," Tom objected. "You're only five."

"I can call. I'm almost six." He started jogging again, heading back for 21 Texasstrasse. He could hope that Tom would follow, but he didn't plan to wait around to find out. If he got picked up, too bad. At least he was alive. The problem now was to get help to Jane before it was too late. And he couldn't go back to the police and fire units clustered by the shed, either; they wouldn't listen to a little girl. They'd take one look at him and bundle him away somewhere, and by the time he got them to listen, Jane Robicheaux would be dead.

CHAPTER
NINETEEN

"If this war is fought, there will be nothing left in Germany to unite. . . ."—Nikita Khrushchev

Tom followed, still limping. Sam wasn't capable of going all that fast himself. His arm was beginning to ache fiercely. Al floated alongside, urging greater speed and muttering to himself and Ziggy, trying to trace the results of the changes caused by Sam's saving Tom. The data was still shifting, as if with every step Sam took something else became the future.

They got to the front door and Sam dug in his pocket for the key. The rising and falling sound of the sirens stuttered and paused. After a moment it took up again, this time in a steady note that lasted a few seconds, paused, repeated itself.

"Listen," Tom said, grabbing at Sam. "Listen!"

Sam yelped and tried unsuccessfully to twist away. "You're hurting me," he pointed out. "Come on, let go. We've got to get upstairs."

Tom ignored him. "The siren stopped. It stopped! That's not the alert any more, it's the All Clear! It's over! It was a drill!"

"Let *go*!" Sam found the key and unlocked the door. It took more effort than he realized to climb the steps, six half-flights to the third floor. Tom was still downstairs, and it didn't seem as if he was going to come back up.

"Better hurry, Sam," Al advised.

Well, perhaps it didn't really matter if Tom showed up or not. He got the key in the door and swung it open.

"Mom!"

The apartment was very still.

"She's in the bedroom," Al said. "Hurry."

Sam hurried.

Jane Robicheaux was lying on the bed, her head turned to one side, her breathing heavy and ragged. She had changed clothes, and was dressed in a lilac dressing gown and had applied fresh lipstick with an unsteady hand; the streak of red trailed from her lips across her cheek like a gash.

"This *is* attempted suicide," Sam said. "She's got to wake up." He leaned over and yelled in the unconscious woman's ear. *"Jane! Jane, wake up!"*

There was no response. Sam climbed up on the bed beside the recumbent woman and turned her head back and forth by the chin. It lolled, offering no resistance, and she didn't blink.

"Sam, something better break soon," Al said. "Ziggy says she's gonna die."

"She is *not* going to die," Sam said grimly, and slapped her.

There was a very faint grunt. "There," Sam said, and hauled off to slap her again, as hard as he could. "Jane! Wake up!"

"Sam, it isn't enough. You've got to call somebody." Al moved around for a better view, standing in the middle of the bed. "How do you know it's suicide?"

"She dressed up to die," Sam explained between his teeth. "Do you mind? I'm trying to save a life here."

"Well, you're not succeeding. You'd better call."

"I'm afraid to stop." He was shaking her now, one-handed, calling to her, refusing to let her slide any deeper into her coma.

"She can't hear you." It was Tom, home at last, standing in the doorway and watching with great interest and no willingness to help. "Did she drink too much?"

"Yes. And she took some pills, and she's going to die if we don't do something."

"Can I hit her?"

Sam looked up incredulously.

"Well, you were," Tom pointed out reasonably. "Why can't I have a turn?"

"I'm trying to wake her up, not hurt her."

"You mean it's for her own good?" Tom said wickedly.

"You ought to give him a shot," Al suggested. "It's only fair, considering what she's done to him. Not to mention what she's done to Missy. And to you."

"Al!" Sam said, horrified.

"Who's Al?" Tom asked.

"It doesn't matter who Al is. Call a doctor."

"Why?" Tom looked slowly from his sister to his mother and back again, challenging. "What will happen if we don't?"

"I don't think he would call a doctor," Al said. "He really does want to see her die."

"No kidding," Sam said, grimly agreeing. "*I'll* call the doctor. Get me the number." He climbed off the bed, brushed by the boy on the way to the living room. Tom stepped forward, and he caught at the boy's shirt. "Don't you hit her," he said. "Don't you hit her just because she hit you. That's not right."

Tom paused. "Can I shake her?" he asked, as if pleading. *C'mon, can't I hurt her a little?*

Sam considered justice and the relative strength of a ten-year-old child, the need to keep the woman from sliding deeper into coma, the memory of the beating over the soft-boiled eggs, and the fact

199

that even he was not always perfect. "Yeah, you can shake her."

He ran into the living room. Al followed behind, pushing buttons on the handlink and reading the data stream. "This is great—"

"I don't care how great it is," Sam said. "I need the number for an ambulance."

"Oh, the number, the hospital number. Yeah." Al pushed a colored cube, read out Ziggy's response. Sam reached for the phone.

"It really is great, Sam," Al went on. "She's going to live, and—and when the ambulance comes by they see Missy, too, and as a result Jane's going to get help. She goes into—" he whistled— *"years* of therapy. Back in the States.

"The major takes early retirement, though. And Missy does grow up to be a psychologist. Specializes in hypnotherapy for victims of child abuse. And Tom has a family, and. . . ."

But there was a voice on the other end of the line by then, and he had given the address, and it was enough. The moment of completeness had arrived. The pieces had fallen into place, he knew it was right, and he Leaped.

He was floating through blue-white light, without sensation, without weight, without flesh, no taste, no scent, in a state of eternal stillness, eternal waiting. He was moving nowhere, doing nothing, only waiting. Time itself, eternity itself, had stopped.

It was almost familiar now, the eternal waiting, the loneliness. He was almost resigned to it. Almost, but not quite. He wanted to go home, but this time, he was certain, there would be no home. He didn't know what he had accomplished, what he had made right. People had lived who once would have died, but he wondered if their living was worth it. He wondered if the changes he made were worth it. They were, after all, changes he had made, not changes they

200

had made for themselves. Did it not matter who changed things in people's lives? And if so, why did he have to be the one to do it?

"Dr. Beckett." The voice again. He never remembered the voice unless he was floating in the light, but once he had returned to the light he remembered and he waited, and it always came.

"Here I am." Here I am, regard me and have pity. He might have felt small, if he had any sense of self at all; the voice was a presence as overwhelming as the light itself. Perhaps the voice and the light were the same. "Why are you doing this to me?"

It was the question he always asked, the question that was never answered. Nor was it answered this time. The presence swept him up and examined him, and suddenly he was filled with a vast feeling of disappointment, of failure.

"It is not complete," the voice said as if pronouncing doom. "It is not enough."

He felt a dreadful weight of despair. It was never enough. He would never be able to do what needed to be done. He was only one person, and there were too many things wrong. And he was tired, so tired of trying. "Please," he whispered. "Please, let me go home."

Wednesday, November 8, 1989
–
Thursday, November 9, 1989

If all it takes for Evil to triumph is for good men to remain silent, then if Good is to overcome those men must speak out . . .

CHAPTER
TWENTY

"The Wall will stand for a hundred years!"
　　　　　　　—Erich Honecker, January 1989

Verbeena Beeks helped the aides settle the body
back into the hospital bed, hooked up the monitors,
and studied the pattern of the brain waves.

"Where is he?" Al said.

Verbeena shook her head. "I don't know, Admiral. We're getting the same readings. His brain is
keeping his body going, but it's just as if there's
nobody home. Even a patient in a coma has *some*
response to outside stimuli. Some part of the brain
will respond, will be aware. What we see here is the
response without the awareness, and I can't begin to
explain it. It isn't supposed to happen this way."

Al let go of a long breath. "I won't ask how long,"
he said. He and Verbeena traded wry glances. One
of the chief mysteries of the Project was where Sam
Beckett went when he was between Leaps. Whatever controlled the process had no regard for the
persons with whom he traded minds; Missy had just
finished another drawing, a sunny, bright picture
filled with hope and small rabbits, when in mid-
word the brown eyes had grown huge and round

and the body of Sam Beckett had collapsed to the floor of the Waiting Room.

Al Calavicci had found himself in the middle of a sentence talking to the blank walls of the Imaging Chamber, his mouth opening and closing like a fish gasping for water. He had shaken his head, grimaced at himself, and hit the controls to open the airlock door. Usually whoever Leaped Sam had better manners than that, but it wasn't the first time a Leap had taken them by surprise.

"Are things better, at least?" Verbeena said. "Poor little girl." Her hand stole across the forehead of the body in the bed, as if in a farewell caress. The body did not move.

"Oh, yeah," Al said. "Her mom got help. Her father retired and started a consulting business." He had left the handlink in the Control Room, was reciting from the last flurry of facts that Ziggy had passed along.

At least history had settled down for a few minutes. As long as Sam was mucking around in Time—or between Time—nothing was predictable. But between Leaps, things stayed quiet. Al had established a pattern; if he was returning to the Project to take a break from his duties as Observer, he would check with Ziggy on any changes the fluxing timelines had made in the Project. But when Sam Leaped, he would come first to the Waiting Room to see if this time the Director had Leaped home.

So far, he hadn't. So Al would then go someplace by himself to find out what had changed this time. This particular time he was hoping for some changes in particular.

"How much more abuse did Missy and her brother have to put up with before her mother was treated?"

Al glanced at the doctor, startled at the level of raw anger in her voice. "None, according to Ziggy. She went into therapy, and the beatings stopped. Of course, it probably helped a lot to have her sent back to the States. In any case, the effects couldn't have been too bad. Missy and Tom have full lives of their own."

"What kind of lives?" Verbeena asked, facing him full on. "Just because Missy has a career doesn't mean she doesn't have emotional scars."

"It doesn't mean she does, either," Al pointed out. "You know as well as I do that it depends as much on the kid as it does on the level of abuse, Verbeena."

Verbeena stopped. Al was relieved to see her blink. He didn't want to have to come right out and remind her that he had suffered an abusive childhood himself, without a home, moved around from one foster home to another, living in an orphanage and finally running away repeatedly. If he did, she might start thinking about what kind of emotional scars *he* carried, and Al Calavicci wasn't about to submit himself to any psychological probing, no sir. He was fine, just fine, thanks. Not a thing wrong with him.

He could see where Missy might be pretty mixed up, even if she looked successful and happy. He just didn't think it would do her any favors to *expect* her to be a mess. People tended to live down to other people's expectations, in his experience.

At least, *he* certainly did.

And it was damned annoying when he ran across somebody who turned out to have higher expectations instead of lower ones. He looked down at the recumbent figure and felt helpless and angry.

"Is he okay?" he said.

"As okay as we know how to make him."

Al sighed. "Okay. I'm going back to my quarters, and then I'll get something to eat. Let me know if . . . anything happens."

"I will," Verbeena assured him.

They both knew it might be minutes, or hours, or even weeks before the body in the bed began showing awareness. Time moved differently between Leaps for Sam than it did for the Project. Al had explained that to him, the very first time the Director had Leaped into that test pilot. It was another one of those mysteries. Al really wished Sam was back to figure it out. He didn't know anybody else who could.

He left the Waiting Room and its attendants behind, taking the long half-finished tunnel to the elevator that would bring him to the living-quarters level. They hadn't quite had the funding to finish this particular area off the way they wanted to, and as a result, it was always chilly, even when the surface was baking hot.

He made his way to the bare room that was his residence in the Project's living quarters and looked around. Nothing had changed.

"Ziggy?" he said.

"Dr. Martinez-O'Farrell is single in this present," Ziggy's disembodied voice said.

Al nodded to himself. Trust the computer to know what was *really* important to him.

"I don't suppose you know . . ."

"No, Admiral. I have no idea where, when, or into whom Dr. Beckett has Leaped." The computer's voice was that of a spoiled, petulant woman. It used to be that of a spoiled, petulant man, but Tina Martinez-O'Farrell had made some adjustments when the computer had begun taking matters into its own microchips and begun expanding its own capabilities beyond anything envisioned by its creator.

Al wasn't sure that anything besides the pitch of its voice had actually changed. Ziggy had been programmed with a will of its own, far too successfully in Al's opinion. Willful didn't begin to describe it at times.

He stripped off his clothes down to his skivvies and stretched out on the bunk, trying to relax. Tina was single, and that was great news. But Sam still hadn't Leaped home. And no progress had been made in identifying the parameters of Leaping.

"Ziggy," he said, his eyes still closed, "what does my schedule look like today?"

"Budget and manpower meetings, testimony for the subcommittee—that's already been prepared— and you have a dinner date with Tina."

Al smirked. The smirk vanished suddenly. "Ah, do I owe her anything? Apologies or anything?"

"No, Admiral. Your relationship with Tina has been extremely positive of late."

Al nodded—a difficult gesture from flat on his back. "Ziggy, how the hell do you keep track?"

The question was greeted with silence.

"Ziggy?"

"I . . . cannot answer the question," the computer said, oddly hesitant.

Al's eyes snapped open. "Why not?"

Another long pause. "The reason . . . appears to be related to the process of Leaping. Whatever the mechanism is that causes Dr. Beckett to Leap appears to have moved us outside of Time for the duration of each Leap. He, and you, and I are the only ones who always coexist both within and outside of time. The Project itself is only in stasis for those moments in which its existence is moot."

"You've said that before."

"I don't know," the computer finally admitted. "I don't have the storage capacity for everything I remember. It isn't possible."

"But it's happening anyway."

"Yes. It seems to be to our benefit, at least."

"I'm glad something about this mess is to some- body's benefit," Al growled. "Is there anything we can do right now?"

"Nothing," the computer admitted even more reluc- tantly.

"Then I'm going to get some sleep. Wake me if . . . you know."

"Yes, Admiral, I know." The lights in the spartan bedroom dimmed. Moments later, Al was snoring.

If he was moving through air, through space, through electronic circuits, there was no way to tell. If time was passing, in either direction, there was no way to tell. And then the voice was gone, and there was the sensation of movement, of rushing through great consequences, of being tossed and torn by something for which he had no name, of being carried once again to a destination he had not chosen, and he was swept up in the moving whirlpool of light, drawn up, up, up, and then down in a dizzying rush, drawn in—

"Missy? Are you all right? You look pale."

CHAPTER
TWENTY-ONE

"The entire East German cabinet, the Communist Party Politburo, and the Central Commit-
tee of the Communist Party have resigned. It
is a change unimaginable only a few months
ago. . . ."

By now he knew what it felt like to Leap out of
someone's life, had learned to recognize the moment
of completeness, of rightness that precipitated the
lunge Out.

But he would never, never learn how to prepare
for the Leap in. He never knew if he would end up in
the body of a pregnant woman, a retarded teenager,
a college professor, or his own best friend. Or even
himself. He never knew if he would find himself
in the middle of giving a college lecture or in the
aftermath of making love, of catching a pop fly or
flying a fighter jet.

But this . . . He looked up into a face he had seen
before, a face with icy blue eyes netted now in subtle
wrinkles; a man tall, thin, athletic, who gave the
impression of being at attention even when holding
out a glass of wine.

"Missy? What the hell is wrong with you now?" The eyes lacked sympathy.

Sam's gaze fell on the proffered glass. It was a cut-crystal goblet, and it was familiar, too. He took it carefully, looking at the hand that accepted it as if he had never seen it before. It was a fine-boned hand, unadorned by jewelry. The nails were neatly trimmed and unpolished.

From another room came shrill giggles, followed by a reprimand in a deep voice, and silence. Sam took a sip of wine to cover a quick survey of his surroundings.

He was standing in the middle of a living room. The painting over the sofa was the same, generic mountains and stream; the sofa was different, newer. A television set in an entertainment unit— his mental calendar automatically added years— was showing a commercial about cornflakes. The sound was muted.

"I'm sorry," he mumbled. *What am I doing?* he thought, not for the first time.

"Are you going to drink that or look at it?" the man muttered.

Sam took another hasty sip, choked as it went down the wrong way. Another man, also tall, thin, and athletic, but a generation younger came into the living room from a side hall. "They're in bed. I told them to settle down. Did you get the cards done?"

He was looking at Sam as he spoke, and Sam got the impression that he was being asked if he had carried out orders. He had no idea what the cards were or if they were done. He coughed to clear his throat. "Um, I'm sure they're okay," he said cautiously.

"They need to go out tomorrow," the older man said.

Sam smiled and nodded, hoping he didn't look as uncertain as he felt.

"I told all the neighbors," the older man said. "They never saw her, of course. She hardly ever left the house."

"Did you set up the flight?" Once again, the younger man directed the question to Sam, who nodded, hoping that his host had taken care of the secretarial details. "I can't afford to be late getting back."

The television shifted to a news report. Dan Rather said something grave and important, and the scene shifted, still mute, to a riot.

Some things were no help in dating a Leap at all.

It hadn't happened before in quite this way. He knew the older man, and he knew the younger man, and he even knew the person he had Leaped into. He was back in Missy Robicheaux, and he had no idea why.

Tom had lived to grow up. The major was hale and hearty, as far as he could see. Which left Jane, Missy's mother.

Sam finished the wine in one gulp, and went looking for the kitchen, ignoring the stares of the two men. As he passed through the hall he paused at the mirror by the front door.

Missy had grown up, too, to be a very pretty woman, perhaps five feet three inches tall. Her hair was short now, brushed back in a style reminiscent of one of Princess Di's, and she wore low-key makeup and delicate gold earrings. She was dressed in a maroon business suit and a white blouse with a frill of lace at the throat. She was the very image of a modern businesswoman. One hand crept up to finger the jabot, tug one edge down. Missy's neck was swanlike. More important, it had no bruises.

On the opposite wall were family pictures. There was one of Missy as a child, taken at about the time Sam had Leaped into her, and another high school graduation picture, paired with one of Tom. He was wearing a uniform. In the background was a shield, embossed with the words, "St. Michael's Military Academy." Between them was a picture of their parents. The major, dressed in a civilian suit, was smiling. Jane had her lips pressed together as if she had bitten something sour. Another picture, of Jane and her sister, looked familiar; it was the one he had seen in the bedroom in the Hainerberg apartment.

He passed the photo gallery and made his way to the kitchen. If anyone had eaten a meal recently, it wasn't obvious. Every surface was spotless. He rinsed the wineglass and set it carefully in the stainless steel sink.

The Door whooshed open behind him. "Sam? You'll never believe this."

"Don't bet on it."

"You've Leaped back into Missy."

"I know that already. Do you have any idea *why*? I thought I was finished with her."

"Well, maybe you are, but somebody else isn't. I guess." Al was dressed in hunter's green, with a vest pinstriped in silver. "When Verbeena told me who was in the Waiting Room, you could have knocked me over with a feather." He was as disappointed as a child at the spoiled surprise.

"I was a little shocked myself. What does Ziggy—"

The conversation was interrupted by Tom, who came out and rattled the cupboards, looking for something and nothing. "Did you see some instant?" he asked at last.

"I'm not sure," Sam responded. He kept silent, waiting for more cues.

"It turns out that Missy really did get that doctorate," Al said. "She's a certified hypnotherapist. Tom here is an electrical engineer, just like Ziggy predicted. Pretty low-level guy, though. Not only is he divorced, but he has trouble getting along with his bosses."

Tom pulled out a small jar and held it out to Sam. "Not too strong, okay?"

Sam didn't understand for a moment. Then he did, and looked at Tom with a new perspective, strongly tinged with distaste. "Thanks," he said deliberately, "but I don't care for any. I think the cups are up there." He gestured at a cupboard over the sink.

Tom blinked in surprise. Before he had a chance to say anything more, Sam turned his back on him and left.

Once out in the hall, he stood uncertainly for a moment, then turned in the direction opposite the way that led back to the living room. He found himself facing a hallway full of doors. The first led to a bathroom; as he opened the second he heard child-voice whispers, quickly stifled.

Edging the door open, he peeked in to find a pair of dark-headed boys lying on a moonlit pillow, their eyes shut just a little too tightly. The light cast odd shadows across the bed. He withdrew and closed the door softly.

"Are they still talking?" Tom said behind him.

"No," Sam said "They look like they're asleep." It was perfectly true.

"Yeah, they *look* like it," Al said. "Those are David and Paul, Tom's boys. Their mother is Jessica. Tom's divorced."

"They'd better be," Tom said. "If you hear anything, let me know." He started back toward the living room.

"And it's November eighth, 1989, and we just aren't sure why you're here and why you've Leaped back into Missy. Ziggy's talking to himself. Herself."

"Itself," Sam muttered, continuing to move down the hall.

"What?" Tom turned back, thinking his sister was addressing him.

"Nothing," Sam reassured him. Tom shrugged and went around the corner.

The next door led to still another bedroom, this one decorated with photographs of jets and a dusty wooden model set up on a dresser. The bed was neatly made, and the closet door stood open, hangers waiting for clothing. A garment bag lay across the bed. It was, Sam guessed, Tom's room.

Opposite, another door stood ajar, and he looked in. By its barrenness it looked like another guest room, but a pair of high heels and a purse beside a suitcase identified its occupant. Sam glared at the heels—Missy was wearing flats at the moment—and settled in a chair to rummage through the purse.

"You're here in time for Jane Robicheaux's funeral tomorrow," Al said. "Tom and the kids came in from Omaha. Missy isn't married. She has a practice in Los Angeles—you're in Portland, Oregon, by the way." He studied the handlink. "It looks like this is the last time the family is together. Missy and Tom have written to each other, but they haven't had any personal contact for the last several years, and none at all after this. The major's still alive, but they haven't any contact with him, either."

A wry smile twisted Missy's features. "I always sort of wondered what happened to people after I Leaped out," Sam said. "Now I know. They just go on living their lives, don't they?"

"But they're *better* lives. I mean, think what would have happened if you hadn't been there."

Sam heaved a sigh. "Right. Okay. What does Ziggy think I'm supposed to do this time?"

"Ziggy doesn't have the foggiest idea."

"Isn't technology wonderful."

"We're working on it."

Sam gave him a look. "Thank you, that's a great help."

"Well, we are." Al could get a lot of mileage out of an injured tone.

Sam looked at the watch on the thin gold chain around his left wrist. "It's only nine o'clock. Do you have any idea what they were talking about, or am I going to have to go in and punt again?"

"Forty-two, seventy-three, sixteen, hut." Al shrugged.

Sam glared at him, wheeled, and headed back into the kitchen.

The major and his son were sitting at the table, sharing a comradely beer and exchanging stories about Jane Robicheaux.

"Do you remember the sash she made you for Boy Scouts?" The major chuckled. "She decided no son of hers was going to wear Army green."

"I had the only Air Force blue sash in the country," Tom laughed awkwardly. "Got a real kick out of it."

Sam paused by the door, listening. "How old were you then?" he asked.

"Oh, what was it, thirteen, fourteen?" the major said.

"I don't really remember." There was a smile on Tom's face, but Sam was watching his hand, gripping the handle of a beer stein. The fingers were white and red. "I was just a kid."

"She made you wear that sash to every meeting," the major laughed.

"Every one," Tom agreed, still smiling.

"She liked her men in uniform," the major went on. "She made sure you had white, long-sleeved shirts and blue slacks just like mine, even when you were just a little kid." His voice quavered a little, and he took a quick drink to hide it.

"They hid the bruises," Sam interrupted, his voice harsh even to his own ears.

The two men looked over in amazement. "They what?" Major Robicheaux said.

"What are you talking about?" Tom said. "What bruises?"

"The marks on your arms," Sam said. "She made you wear long sleeves to hide them."

"What the hell are you talking about?" Tom said. "What bruises?"

217

He was staring at his sister as if trying to tell her something with the intensity of his gaze alone.

"What the hell d'you mean?" the major echoed.

Sam looked from one to the other. "The bruises. From where she hit us."

Tom closed his eyes. "Oh, God. Not that again."

"What?" The major was beginning to sound like a broken record. "What bruises?"

Sam stared at him, aghast. He could remember, even through the swiss-cheesing of his Leap, saluting this man, holding his hand straight, not cupped, to a face that had just been beaten black and blue. Hadn't he seen? Didn't he even notice? Or had he really believed the excuse about "tripping" and "clumsy" that Jane Robicheaux had offered?

"She's a psychologist, Dad," Tom said, his voice thick with scorn. "She's got to analyze everything. She thinks that a spanking is some big deal."

"It is some big deal," Sam began.

Tom interrupted. "Why don't you just shut up about that stuff? For God's sake, the woman is dead. Your mother is *dead!* You don't have to smear her even in her grave, do you?"

"I'm not—" Sam began.

"I don't think I want to hear any more of this," the major said with finality. He got up from his chair, moving as if his joints ached. New wrinkles etched themselves across his face. He looked at Sam and at Tom, and shook his head. "Your mother loved you. You just remember that. She loved you a lot."

They watched him go in silence, listening to his footsteps down the hall, the soft grunts of age, the fumblings of sound as he opened his bedroom door and reached for the light and shut the confrontation away from him.

"I hope you're happy, dammit," Tom growled at last. "I told you once already I didn't want to get your letters if you had to go on and on about Mom.

You'd think you could let up. It wasn't that big a deal."

"Is that what you think?"

"That's what I *know*," Tom emphasized, slapping the table. "So shut up, understand. I'm sick of you making up lies about her."

"Were they lies?" Sam said. He wondered what was in the letters Missy had written. She might have lied, he supposed.

"Damn right they were lies, and you know it! And if you tell Dad—if you hurt him any more, I'm . . . I'm . . ."

"She hit us—" Sam began.

He didn't expect the reaction the words evoked. Tom lunged around the table, coming directly for him.

"Shut up! Shut up, dammit! I don't want to hear it! I don't want to hear one more word about this, do you hear me! She did not hit us! You're making it up! It's not true!"

Involuntarily, Sam stepped back, away from the rage in the other man's voice. He found himself lifting one hand as if to placate Tom, and dropped it. There was no placating him; he was on his feet and coming toward Sam, his face flushed, his eyes almost black. He looked completely out of control, wild with rage.

In trying to give him space, Sam was backed against the counter. He reached inside himself to find the quiet place that he would need to defend himself—

—and Tom stopped, an inch short of outright assault, baffled by Sam's silence. He towered over Sam, his face working, and did an abrupt about-face. "Get the hell out of here," he said. "Just get away from me."

"Sounds like a good idea to me," Al commented. It was a good thing that Tom was facing in the other direction; Sam glared at his Observer, who gave him an innocent look and jerked a thumb toward the doorway. When Sam hesitated, Al waggled his eyebrows and jerked his thumb again. "Thattaway, Sam."

Giving Tom's back one last glance, Sam followed him.

CHAPTER

TWENTY-TWO

"The borders between East and West, locked in
an Iron Curtain for more than thirty years, have
been opened to immigration . . ."   —May 1989

"I know you," Missy Robicheaux said to Verbeena
Beeks. "Have we met before?"

"I'm not sure," Verbeena said warily.

"At a conference, perhaps? I'm Dr. Robicheaux."

There was a moment before Verbeena could gath-
er her wits to take the hand held out to her, and in
that moment Missy's gaze fell on the hand she was
holding out, and she screamed.

This part, at least, Verbeena was used to. "Ziggy!"
she snapped, stepping away from the other woman.
"Class three!"

Obediently, the computer directed a puff of color-
less gas from an invisible vent under which the Visitor was standing. It wasn't something they liked to
do—it was the same body getting gassed every time,
and after a while the effects would add up—but
sometimes it was necessary. They'd had to install
it after a few Visitors tried to become violent.

Class three, at least, merely calmed things down
a little. Verbeena waited until she felt the fan at

her back dissipating the remainder of the chemical, and stepped forward again, taking Sam Beckett's hand in hers. "I know this is frightening," she began soothingly.

Missy was looking around at the white room with the white walls and the Observation room at the top of the steps, at the little table they hadn't gotten around to moving out after the last Leap, at Verbeena, wide-eyed.

"It's a dream," she murmured, her voice betraying her confusion. "This is the same dream I had when I was a little girl. The very same dream. You were in it then, and you're in it now. And I'm in another body. In a man's body.

"It's a reaction," she said dreamily, a smile beginning to appear on her face. "Reaction formation to a feeling of helplessness engendered by re-exposure to the familial environment. And my unconscious belief that men are better able to cope expresses itself in my being in a man's body." She frowned. "I thought I got over that." She reconsidered. "I could write a paper about this."

"At least somebody could," Verbeena muttered, guiding the woman over to the bed.

"Oh look, it's the same bed and everything." She looked up at Verbeena. "You were my guardian angel, before. Are you this time, too? Is this going to be a good dream?"

"Oh, absolutely, honey, you bet," the doctor answered as she settled her in. *I certainly hope so. Sam! Will you quit getting into these messes!*

"He looked like he was gonna kill you," Al said. "Musta got that temper from his mother."

They were in the bathroom again, a pleasant enough room decorated in green. A bar of deodorant soap in a seashell soap dish sat next to a sink with gold and plastic faucets. It seemed as if at least once every Leap he and Sam had a conference in a bathroom, usually not nearly as nice as this one. It wasn't so bad when Sam Leaped into a man, but in his heart of hearts, Al did feel the least bit uneasy when Sam was in a woman's body and they were in the bathroom together. There was just something a little too strange about it.

"Yeah, he did," Sam said. "So? What have you got?"

Al shrugged. "*Nada*."

"Na-da? NA-da? What do you mean, '*nada*'?"

Al took a deep breath, removed his cigar, and said again, "Nada. Nothing. Zilch. The nearest thing Ziggy can figure is, you haven't finished yet. That's happened before."

"Not really," Sam protested. "Except one—I can't remember. Something about a rifle—"

Al chomped down on the cigar again, refusing to be drawn. Ziggy had postulated that there was probably a very good reason for Sam to have these holes in his memory, and Al wasn't about to fill them in if he didn't have to. Especially holes relating to previous Leaps. He seemed to retain the information he needed about Missy, though, so it was probably safe enough to talk to him about that one. Of course, Ziggy also postulated that there was a very good reason for him to Leap into Missy Robicheaux twice, and the computer couldn't figure that one out either.

"The funeral is in the morning." Al took control of the conversation again. "The day after that, Tom and the kids go home, and so do you."

"Leaving the major here?"

Al nodded. "He's got friends and stuff here. He's okay. Still kicking, even in our time. A little slower, maybe. And so is Tom, and so is Missy. Nobody dies this time. They just don't get together again."

"Well, that makes for a nice switch. Their not dying, I mean." Sam leaned back against the bathroom counter and crossed his arms.

Al cocked his head, watching him. "Doesn't that feel funny?"

"What?"

"You know." Al mimed crossing his arms, holding them well away from his chest. Sam looked down at the arms pressed against his—Missy's—breasts.

"Oh. That. No. I don't even notice any more."

"*I* would," Al muttered. No matter how many times it happened, he couldn't get over the idea of a man being in a woman's body. It didn't seem right somehow.

"I'll bet you would," Sam agreed. "Can we get back to the point here, please? Isn't Ziggy going to quote me odds on *something*?"

Al shook his head and slapped at the handlink, which squealed in token protest. "Nope. Not a thing."

"Al, how am I supposed to Leap out of here if I don't change something?" There was a tinge of desperation in Sam's voice. "Am I going to spend the rest of my life as Missy Robicheaux?"

"Damfino." The two friends stared at each other helplessly.

"Then you don't think anything's going to happen tonight, either?"

Al shook his head.

"Then go pound some data out of Ziggy for me. I'm going to bed."

Al opened his mouth.

Sam forestalled him. "No, you can*not* watch me get undressed."

The Observer managed a look of offense at the mere suggestion, opened the Door, and left.

Some part of Sam wasn't the least bit surprised when he was awakened at the crack of dawn by the sounds of people moving around. Fortunately or otherwise, he had become more than familiar with sunrise as a boy working on a farm.

"Mass is at eight A.M. sharp," the major called

through the bedroom door. "It's six. Let's get going."

What, no "eight hundred hours"? Sam thought, as he brushed his teeth and put on makeup. Not bad, he thought, inspecting the results. It was a good thing that Missy didn't wear much to begin with. He really hated messing with mascara and eyeliner— he felt as if he was going to poke himself in the eye every time.

Underwear was no longer a problem; sometimes he thought he could trade pantyhose tips with transvestites, make a new career out of it, in fact, if the quantum physics thing didn't pan out. Of course, if it didn't, that meant he was stuck, and he wouldn't be a transvestite, exactly. Transsexual?

No, dammit. He was Sam Beckett. If Leaping had taught him anything, it was that the important thing was the person you were inside, not outside. It was the person inside who counted. It really didn't matter if you were male or female, black or red or white, a super-genius or mildly retarded; what mattered was the kind of human being you were. It was, he sometimes thought, the whole point of Quantum Leaping.

He found a dark green dress hanging in the closet, decided that it was acceptable for a funeral, and put it on. The next problem was the shoes. Gritting his teeth, he slid his feet in and practiced walking back and forth on the bedroom carpet, trying to let the body's reflexes control his stride. It was tricky. The body might know how to walk in the damned things, but in his own mind he was certain no human being was supposed to walk at a constant tilt like that. He would *never* get used to high heels.

As ready as he'd ever be, he wobbled out to the kitchen and met the two men and the twin boys. David and Paul were about seven, too old to perceive him as Sam Beckett; he greeted them gravely. They both had violet eyes and dark brown hair, family traits shared by their father and aunt. In their case,

225

their hair was slicked back hard, still showing the furrows of combs, and they were identically dressed in blue suits, miniature versions of their father's. Something about them echoed the mirror portrait of their grandmother and great-aunt, who were twins as well. Twinning skipped a generation, as Sam recalled.

"Hands?" their father demanded.

They held out their hands, pink with scrubbing, turning them palm-up, palm-down to demonstrate their cleanliness.

"That'll do."

Sam thought he caught a shared glance between the two, but it was too quick to interpret.

The major was dressed in a dark charcoal-gray suit, with a gold-buttoned vest and spotless, faultlessly ironed white shirt. His cuff links matched his vest buttons. He wore the suit as if it were a uniform.

Looking at him, Sam could not detect any visible signs of grief. Steven Robicheaux looked at his watch. "Let's get this show on the road, shall we?" he said.

It was an odd way to refer to one's wife's funeral, to say the least. If Sam hadn't seen the expression on the man's face the night before, he might have believed the occasion meant nothing to him.

They piled into a sedan, Sam in between the two boys in the back, Tom and the major in front, and drove through a typical late-fall morning. The boys exclaimed at the first bridge they passed over, until a sharp word from their father silenced them. Thereafter they looked out the windows and leaned forward, once they realized Sam didn't mind, to trade looks and point out new sights in perfect silence.

The church wasn't like the American chapel. The only thing it appeared to have in common with the place Sam had last attended Mass, in fact, was the holy water font just inside the front door. The altar was at the apex of three fans of pews divided by two wide aisles; behind it an abstract stained glass window stretched upward to the heavens, casting blue and yellow and green shadows across the few other people making up the congregation for this Thursday-morning service.

They filed into the first pew on the far right. Before them, a brass casket rested on a bier. Sam made sure he was on the end, and waited for Al to show up. At least, he thought, he had gone through this Mass business once before, and he could remember the gestures and responses.

The priest's entrance disabused him of that notion. Comparing this service to the one he had been through before, he found it difficult to identify the similarities. The prayers were in English, not Latin, the priest was facing the wrong way, and the translations were fluid. There didn't seem to be as much kneeling, either.

Al showed up halfway through. Sam made a discreet face at him; Al shrugged. "Hey, this is a modern Mass, Sam. I don't know it any better than you do."

His voice was still a whisper, though, Sam noted. You could take the libertine out of the Church, perhaps, but not the Church out of the libertine.

It was not only a modern Mass, but not much of a funeral. There was no sermon. In the middle of the service, the priest and the two altar boys came over to cense the casket, the smoking gold thurible swinging back and forth and crosswise, leaving the air thick with burning perfume.

He managed to make it through, nonetheless. This time the priest dismissed them in English: "Go, the Mass is ended."

They left with the smell of incense still clinging to their clothing. Sam took deep breaths to clear the scent from his lungs. The major didn't pause to speak to the priest afterward.

"I want to clear out some of the insurance things and the clothing," he said. "Let's get back to the house and take care of that, and then we can go to lunch."

"Have the boys eaten?" Sam inquired. He wasn't particularly bothered at the prospect of missing breakfast, but he wondered at the casual dismissal of the children's needs.

Both the major and Tom looked surprised. "They can wait," Tom snapped. "We have things to do."

"They can *not* wait," Sam responded firmly. "I'll feed them."

The chill this evinced remained until they returned to the house. The major kept his feelings about insubordination almost to himself. Tom shrugged, indifferent. By the time they got back to the house, feeding the children was uppermost on the agenda. Sam herded the boys into the kitchen and began making cinnamon toast.

"What about eggs?" the major suggested.

Sam flinched and shook his head. "No, thanks. Unless you've got a poacher, and like them hard enough to nail to the wall. I've got a thing about eggs."

"Suit yourself." The major looked around, vaguely dissatisfied. "When you get finished, there's a trunk of your mother's you need to go through. See if there's anything you want in there. The rest of it we'll get rid of. Give it to charity or something."

Sam winced, wondering if there was anything he should save for Missy. Now there was a reason, as if he needed one, for getting out of here quickly: to let her choose her memories of her mother.

Though come to think of it, perhaps she would best like to have no memories at all.

The trunk was shoved into the back of a walk-in closet, as if it contained useless things, things which would never be called for but were too good to throw away. Sam wrestled it out of its corner and pried open the lid.

Two pairs of violet eyes peered over his shoulders.

"Oh," one of the boys said—Sam thought it might be Paul, though to be honest he couldn't really tell them apart. "That's just paper and junk. There isn't any good stuff."

Sam tossed him a grin. The trunk contained a length of Irish linen tablecloth; lifted away, it revealed a layer of several cardboard boxes and manila folders. He lifted out one of the folders, paging through it at random. It contained recipe clippings and notes on sewing patterns. The first two boxes contained dusty, very much out-of-style shoes. The boys, bored, wandered out of the room.

He continued to burrow. Another folder held report cards for Missy and Tom, dating back to nursery school. Still another contained all the bills for therapy received, beginning in September 1961 and continuing for the next twelve years. Tucked in on top was a notation on Missy's broken arm, with a note from the doctor indicating the patient could not recall how the injury had happened.

One of the boxes contained black-and-white and color photographs in various stages of brittleness, including pictures of Missy's and Tom's graduations, hoodings, and robings from the eighth grade through doctorate—Missy's, at least; Tom didn't seem to have gone past the MS.

There were other things in the boxes, too. He sorted, stacked, and eventually returned almost everything to the trunk, unable to decide what to keep and what to throw away.

But there was one item he kept out. He'd show it to Tom, he decided. Maybe it would help. Help what, he wasn't sure.

CHAPTER
TWENTY-THREE

"Nothing will be the same again."
                    —Willy Brandt, November 1989

He came out of the bedroom and into the living room to find Tom staring down at his sons, a look of utter disgust on his face. Sam could see why. The once-pristine blue suits were rumpled and dirty, and one of the boys had torn a hole in the knee of his pants.

"I can't believe you didn't have the sense to change clothes," their father was saying bitterly.

"We were playing," one of the boys said.

"Don't you talk back to me! Damn you, don't you talk back to me!" He raised his hand, and Sam moved forward to prevent the blow. But he stopped himself; seeing the lift of the boys' heads when they caught sight of Sam moving in, he turned around.

"Can you believe these kids?" he said wearily. "Look at them. They'll never be able to wear those suits again."

"They'd probably grow out of them before they had the chance," Sam said, watching him carefully.

"Don't make excuses for them. They come up with plenty of their own. They're always talking back. I can't believe it. You and I never talked back the way these kids do."

Sam, who had never heard the kids in question talking back, and remembering all too vividly what happened when Missy and Tom had done so, held his peace.

"Have you seen the news?" he asked instead. "They're tearing down the Berlin Wall."

Tom nodded. Then, almost as an afterthought, he turned back to the boys. "You're dismissed. Go get cleaned up and changed. And I don't ever want to see you playing in your good clothes again. Not ever, do you understand me?"

"Yes, sir," the two mumbled in chorus, and took off at a dead run.

Tom looked after them, shaking his head and running his hand through his hair. "Honest, I don't know what to do with those kids sometimes. Maybe they would have been better off with their mother after all. Though she never heard of discipline. Lets them run wild every time they go visit. It's hell getting them squared away again once I get them back. Going back and forth is hard on kids."

Sam nodded. "Um, Tom, could we talk about that a little?"

Tom laughed. "What, is my baby sister the psychologist going to teach me how to raise my kids now?"

"Do you really not remember how Mom used to beat us?"

Tom's face became a mask. "I remember she was strict with us. There's nothing wrong with that. Kids have to learn to respect their parents."

"She was more than strict. Don't you remember how she hit me the morning of the alert, when I didn't eat a soft-boiled egg fast enough?" Behind Tom, he could see the Door slide upward, and Al come out to join them.

"He wasn't there for that," Al said. "He was still

in his room, packing to run away. But don't let that stop you, Sam, you're on the right track."

"No," Tom said, tightlipped. "I remember telling you I didn't want to talk about this stuff anymore, though."

"Don't you remember helping me clean up the mess that day? That was the day you ran away. That was the day I broke my arm. The day Mom—" he stumbled, realizing suddenly that Tom might very well never have been told that his mother had tried to kill herself. He wasn't sure whether using a euphemism at this point would help or hurt matters. "The day Mom took the pills and liquor," he said, opting for the exact truth, "and we had to call the ambulance."

"I remember when she got sick," Tom said. "But not the rest of it. I don't think the rest of it ever happened. You're just making all this stuff up, using it as an excuse not to get married and have a family." He shook his head. "This psychology crap of yours never did anybody any good. Mom or anybody."

"It probably kept her from killing her daughter," Sam said, his voice very soft. "You really don't remember, do you? You've blocked it all out."

"Well, either I've blocked it all out or it never happened to begin with," Tom responded sharply. "And since I seem to be doing okay with my life, I know which answer I think is right."

"Yeah? You're not doing all that okay," Al jeered. "You got divorced, you got fired, you lost a promotion at your last job. Real okay, huh?"

"Do you remember this?" Sam said, holding out what he had been carrying, what he had found in one of the boxes in the trunk, carefully preserved.

Something flickered in Tom's expression as he took the model biplane in his hands, turning it around and around, carefully, as if examining the workmanship. "What's this, one of my old toys? Where did you dig this up?"

"It was in the trunk. Mom saved it. Are you sure you don't remember? This is the one that got broken the day you ran away. She saved it. She tried to fix it. Look." There was a glob of glue, inexpertly applied, on one wing, holding it to the body of the plane.

Tom bit his lower lip and shook his head. "Nope. It's a broken toy. God knows we've got enough of them back at the house. Those kids can't keep their toys in one piece. You planning on keeping this?"

"I was hoping you would," Sam answered quietly, beginning to lose hope. He had really believed that the sight of the little biplane, so carefully preserved for so long, would have evoked the memories in Tom, so that he would see the connections between what he was doing to his sons and what had been done to him, so many years ago.

"It isn't enough," Al said. "He really has buried it deep."

The Observer and the Project Director watched as Tom Robicheaux tossed the toy into a convenient wastebasket. "Does this conclude our session?" he asked. "Send your bill to my office, little sister. And quit bugging me about it, okay? I've had just about enough of your fantasies of being beaten. You're the sick one, if you ask me."

"I'm open to suggestions," Sam said later, talking to Al in the back bedroom. He had excused himself from dealing with Tom and the major, telling them he was going to sort clothing. Meanwhile, he'd rescued the model from the wastebasket and was trying in vain to straighten a warped strut. "I really thought seeing this would have made him remember."

"Maybe he does remember," Al suggested. "He just doesn't want to admit it. Missy says she's afraid he's going to go the same route Jane did. Carrying abuse forward another generation. It happens

234

a lot. Most child abusers were abused themselves, she says. They don't think it's abuse because that's what they grew up with. They think it's normal discipline."

"I can't believe anybody really thinks that hitting a kid is the right way to discipline him."

"You never got spanked when you were a kid?"

"Well, yeah, once or twice, but only when I deserved it."

"Jane only hit her kids when they deserved it, too," Al pointed out. "It's all in the eye of the beholder. Or in the standards you grew up with."

"I wasn't abused," Sam said, swift to the defense of his parents. "I knew my parents loved me."

"Nobody said they didn't. But one or two spankings over a childhood isn't the same thing Tom and Missy grew up with before Jane went into therapy."

"So what happened, did she find a magic bullet and quit, just like that?" Sam was getting frustrated.

"There *aren't* any magic bullets. But she learned to control herself once she realized what she was doing. She loved her kids, too. Just like Tom loves his."

Sam nodded, recalling the folders and pictures. "So what am I supposed to do?"

"You've already figured it out," Al informed him. "You're here to break the chain of abuse. To stop Tom before he really gets started. Otherwise those kids are going to be damaged the same way he was, and it's never going to end."

"How am I supposed to do that when he won't even admit he was abused? He doesn't even want to talk about it!"

Al shrugged. "You got me," he said. "I thought the model airplane would do it, myself."

"Does Ziggy have any ideas?"

"Sam, if you're out of ideas, and I'm out of ideas, it

isn't very likely that Ziggy's going to be able to come up with anything. I mean, he's smart, but he's still a computer."

"What about Missy? What about Verbeena?"

"Verbeena says that if an abuser acknowledges the problem, that's more than half the battle. Tom just won't, that's all."

"I wish you could play back for him that day," Sam murmured. "He may think he's forgotten it, but I'll bet he hasn't. I don't see how anybody could possibly forget something like that."

"He hasn't forgotten it, he's denied it ever happened." Al pecked at the handlink. "Maybe if we could do a hologrammatic light show for him—Nope. Ziggy says it won't work. I don't know how you're going to do it, Sam. But Ziggy says that you've got to find some way, or you aren't going to be able to Leap."

Dinner that evening was an uneasy meal. Sam realized early on that Missy's father and brother expected the woman in the house to take care of the meal, so he took the boys into the kitchen with him and made spaghetti, ignoring the futile attempts by Al to taste the sauce and offer culinary criticism. They were good at setting the table, only having to go back once for the right number of place settings. A massive china cabinet in the dining room held the crystal and china he remembered, but he opted to use instead the more workaday, modern almost-china and plastic glasses from a cupboard over the dishwasher.

He set David to tearing lettuce for salad, and Paul to peeling carrots, while he set water to boil for the pasta.

"You aren't really going to use one of those mixes for the sauce, are you?" Al mourned. "Sam, all you gotta do is get some fresh oregano. . . ."

Sam, unable to respond because of the presence of

the twins, closed his eyes and thought dark thoughts. Despite the dubious assistance of the hologram, the chef and his assistants managed to put together a reasonable facsimile of a meal. Al finally gave up and returned to the Project to fix an Italian meal of his own—"*without* using one of those damn mixes," as he informed Sam.

The major and Tom appeared to approve. They ate, at least, with every evidence of enjoyment.

"A round of applause for Paul and David," Sam insisted, as Tom polished off the last piece of homemade garlic bread. "I couldn't have done it without them."

"We did the salad all by ourselves," David said shyly.

"Well, I think you did a damn fine job," the major growled, and applauded as directed. After a moment Tom joined in, and Sam looked at the boys' glowing faces. How could Tom see this, and not understand the difference between this and the lack of expression his sons habitually wore? He thought they respected him. Sam called it fear.

"So you're going to grow up to be chefs and wear white hats?" Tom jibed. "You'll look pretty silly."

"We won't be silly," Paul said.

"If I say you're silly, you're silly." It sounded like a joke, but it wasn't. The major stopped clapping and looked at his son.

But he said nothing. He saw what was going on, Sam realized, just as he had seen bruises twenty-eight years before. But he was willing to accept those bruises as the result of an accident then, and he was going to let Tom's remark pass as a joke now.

And Sam was trapped too, because if he made an issue of it now, it would exaggerate the entire incident out of proportion. But he had to say something. "You might *look* silly," he offered, "but you'd still be very good chefs."

The instant the words were out of his mouth he was disgusted with himself. Surely he could have come up with something more devastating to Tom, more supportive to the children?

He'd probably think of something, three Leaps from now.

Meanwhile the boys were giving him grateful glances and Tom was shaking his head to himself.

They finished dinner, and the men moved into the living room to continue talking about world events and football, while Sam and the boys remained behind to clean up. Paul scraped carrot peelings and other salad scraps into the disposal, while David rinsed the dishes and put them in the dishwasher. Sam finally realized he was in the way, and stood back to let them work.

"You do this all the time at home?" he asked.

"Yes," they chorused. "Is something wrong?" David added, standing in the middle of the kitchen floor with a plate in his hands. "We're doing it right. Aren't we?"

"Sure you are," Sam reassured him. "You're doing it fine."

They finished up, and he sent them back into their room to play with some toy trucks. He paused at the door to the living room, listening to the conversation about Gorbachev and Honecker, *perestroika* and *glasnost*, the opening of international borders, the fall of the Wall. He could remember being involved in conversations like that, years ago, when he worked on Star Bright.

But he had no desire to become involved in a discussion of them now, and they showed no inclination to invite him to participate anyway. The major glanced up and said, "I could use another cup of coffee, hon," and went on talking.

Sam took the cup back to the kitchen, refilled it, and brought it back. He sat in one of the armchairs, slipped off his shoes, and pulled his legs up under him—a very comfortable posture in this body. The conversation continued. He made one or two contributions, largely unnoticed. After a while Al showed up again, took in the situation, and claimed a corner of the couch opposite the major, adding a running commentary of his own. The information that Ziggy hadn't come up with anything new was incidental.

The major didn't want his children to leave in the morning, Sam could tell. He was pouring out months of conversation, observation, instructions meant to show that he was still the Father, still an important man in his house. But as it got later, he began to fade, and he finally caught himself stifling a yawn and abruptly decided to go to bed.

Sam and Tom and Al remained, sharing a few moments of peace and quiet, Tom finishing his coffee and Sam trying frantically to think of a way to convince the man to deal with the past before he left Portland and the influence of his sister forever, Al polluting the atmosphere of the Imaging Chamber with a good cigar and vast contentment.

"You ought to do this more often," the Observer informed Sam. "It's been a long time since we've had a bull session like this one."

Sam blinked, exasperated. He couldn't respond directly. And there were more important issues to deal with.

"They're good boys," he said at last.

Tom smiled. "You aren't going to start again, are you?"

Sam's skin crawled. The threat was implicit in the words, not the tone. It was as if that pattern of words had been used before, innumerable times, and each time the incident ended in violence.

And each time . . . he wondered. How could Tom *not* remember? How deeply barricaded *were* those memories that it was so desperately important that he not let out?

He got up and went into the bedroom, retrieving

239

the toy airplane and bringing it back to the living room where Tom still sat.

Al saw the model and the expression on Sam's face. "Uh, oh. You've got an idea, don't you?"

Sam smiled grimly. Maybe Ziggy couldn't play it back for Tom—but he, Sam Beckett, didn't have a photographic memory for nothing. And he, Sam Beckett, was the only one who *could* play it back. Because *he had been there*.

"I don't like the looks of this," Al said.

Neither did Tom. "What the hell is that for?" he said. "I told you that subject was closed."

"I know what you said," Sam answered. He set the model down on the coffee table between them, propping up the broken strut so it looked whole. "You really don't remember how this happened?"

Tom looked at the model and shrugged. "Stepped on it, probably."

Sam thought about it, nodded. "Something like that." He leaned forward in his chair, placed both feet flat upon the floor.

"Don't you remember what your room looked like in Hainerberg?" he said. It was there before him, as if a picture in stereoscope, the gift of a photographic memory when there weren't any holes. "You had model planes hanging from the ceiling. You had a Fokker and a Mosquito and a bomber, a B-52, and one of those big transport planes I never knew the name of. Remember?"

Tom shifted uneasily, shaking his head. "So? Every kid had planes."

"You had airplanes on your bedspread. With pictures of pilots wearing red silk scarves and wearing goggles. Remember, Tom? And you had one of those rugs, a shag rug, and it had an airplane on it—what kind of plane was on the rug?"

"A Messerschmidt. It was a German design. Mom made it up for me."

Sam nodded. "Yeah. Messerschmidt." He reached

240

out with one finger and touched the wing of the wooden model. "But *you* built the others. The ones hanging from the ceiling, and the ones on the table, the finished ones you didn't have time to hang up yet. The room smelled like glue, airplane glue. You spent a lot of time on it, didn't you? Building those planes was a lot of fun."

"Yeah, so?"

"It took a lot of time. A lot of effort. Didn't it? Can you remember how careful you had to be . . ."

"Oh, will you cut it out! Yeah, I was careful! I was a kid! It was a kid's hobby! So what!" He started to get to his feet.

"*So what,*" Sam said, his voice as low and as ugly and as much like that of Jane Robicheaux, that long-ago Monday afternoon, as he could make it. "*Don't you talk to me in that tone of voice.*"

Tom flinched back. "What—"

With a sweep of his right hand, Sam knocked the model off the table, sending it crashing into the wall, and got to his feet, standing over the man on the couch. "*Don't you talk back to me! Damn you, don't you talk back to me! You little ungrateful monster! Monster!*

"All you wanted was something to eat," Sam went on, in his own voice, but still shouting, still chipping away. "You were late. Daddy came home and left again, we had dinner and you weren't there, all you wanted was something to eat! Remember? *Remember?*" He stepped away long enough to snatch up the pieces of the model, thrust it under the man's nose. "You were working on this model. *This* model!"

His voice changed again to the pitch and texture Jane Robicheaux had used, so many years ago. "You came home late. *Your father was here for dinner!* " he screamed at the man on the couch. " *Your father was here and you weren't home! He called you and you didn't come! Where were you? You lazy, useless, disobedient boy! You don't deserve to have a father!*

You don't deserve to have a family!' Isn't that what she said to you that day? Isn't it? And she said, *'Don't you ever do what you're told!'* and you said, 'All I wanted was something to eat! What are you going to do, starve me?'

"And then what happened? What happened, Tom? What came next? You remember, don't you? What came next?"

"She hit me," he said, shrinking back into the cushions. "She hit me, and she knocked the models down, and she broke it. She hit me into the wall and she broke it—"

"And then what happened?" Sam said inexorably, hammering at him. "What happened next, Tom?"

"I—hit—her—back—and I ran away," he gasped. "I ran away, and then there was the alert, and the fire, and you came—"

"Why did you run away, Tom? Why did you run away?"

"Because she hit us, and she yelled at us, and she called us names!" Tom was crumbling, caught up in the memory Sam was *being* for him, playing back for him.

"And it hurt, didn't it?" He couldn't let up now. Not yet. Out of the corner of his eye he could see Al, burning cigar forgotten, staring at him with his mouth open, and he could tell that the major was standing in the doorway just outside the periphery of his vision. "It *hurt*, didn't it!"

"I was bad!" Tom wailed, weeping openly now. "I didn't check in! I talked back! I deserved it!"

"No," Sam said, in an almost normal voice now. His throat hurt. It didn't matter. He was breaking through. "You did *not* deserve it. If you remember what happened to you, you remember what happened to me, too. Neither one of us deserved it. No kids deserve that kind of treatment. We didn't deserve it then, and your kids don't deserve it now."

"I—I don't hit my kids," Tom gasped.

"Neither did your mother, to begin with," Al and Sam said at almost exactly the same time, and traded a startled glance.

"It doesn't start with hitting," Sam went on. "It starts with yelling. And you are yelling *exactly the same things* at your boys that your mother yelled at you, twenty-eight years ago. You almost hit them this afternoon for tearing their clothes. Can you see this? Damn it, Tom, can you see it now?"

He wouldn't look up at Sam, but he looked at the broken pieces of the model, took them up in his hands, and he nodded. "She said those things to us," he whispered. "That's how I learned to say them too. Those are the words you say." His gaze shifted then, and he met his sister's eyes. "I remember. It happened just that way. I remember."

"No," the major said from the doorway. "No. I don't believe it. You're making it up. You're lying."

He faced his children and he denied it, denied his son's tears, his daughter's unfamiliar rage.

"You saw my face when you came home that day," Sam said. "You saw."

"You fell into the coffee table. You were always falling into things."

"I was *pushed*. I was *slapped*. I was hit with a closed fist. I was thrown against the wall."

"Liar." There was utter loathing and condemnation in the old man's tone. "Liar."

"No. I am not a liar."

"She's not lying," Tom said. "She's not. I remember."

"Liar," the old man repeated. "I want you to get out of my house. I want you to go away and never come back. Your mother loved you. She never hit you."

"Jane Robicheaux loved her children," Sam said with precision. "She loved them desperately. And she was in terrible, terrible pain. And as a result she abused them every day, verbally and physical-

243

ly. She cut them down with words as well as with blows. She told them they were stupid, that they were worthless. She hit them and told them it was their fault for getting hit. And because they were kids *they believed her*, and now Tom is doing the same things to his children, the children that he loves, because he was taught that that's the way you love someone. *And I want to see it stop now*."

"Liar," the old man repeated, and turned his back on him.

"He's never going to believe you," Tom said. "He wouldn't see it then and he won't believe it now."

"The point is, do *you*? Are you going to get help?"

"That stuff you were talking about in your letters?"

"Exactly that stuff," Sam agreed. "Are you going to do it?"

Tom looked down at the model in his hands. "I love my kids." He caught back a sob, startling himself. "I love my kids."

That was it. The moment of completeness. Of rightness. Of redemption.

"Bingo," Al said.

And Sam Leaped.

AUTHOR'S NOTE

The American housing development of Hainerberg, Germany, is a real place. Street names in Hainerberg did consist of state names combined with the German word for "street"—thus, "Texasstrasse" is a real street, and the apartment building described did (and still may) exist. American dependents living in Hainerberg and elsewhere in the Federal Republic of Germany in the late fifties and early sixties did keep bags packed and ready in case international tensions exploded and evacuation was required on short notice.

The author is not, however, aware of any actual evacuation alert or drill taking place in Wiesbaden on the date, or during the time period, described. The Robicheaux family is fictional, and any resemblance to any real family living in Hainerberg at that time or at that address is purely coincidental.

The quotations that head the chapters are either from actual documents provided by the American military to its dependents, or from the public record of the time.